Tracy was quiet for a . . . brother started back dow . . . the cabin. Her blond eyebrows drew together over her eyes in concentration. "What do you think of him, Colin?"

"He's sure pretty."

"And he'll probably get even prettier when he gets bigger. You know what I wish?" She sighed. "That I could keep him for my very own horse."

"You can't do that, Tracy!" Colin swung his head around to stare at her. "Dad would *never* let you."

"I know," Tracy said sadly. "We can only keep him until his leg heals and he can go back to the wild. But it's nice to dream about. Think of all the fun we could have."

"Yeah . . ." Colin's voice had grown wistful too.

Again Tracy sighed. If only Whitestar were hers to keep, and if only her father didn't hate mustangs anymore, how wonderful everything would be!

Other Skylark books you will enjoy
Ask your bookseller for the books you have missed

ANNE OF GREEN GABLES by L. M. Montgomery

DAPHNE'S BOOK by Mary Downing Hahn

FELITA by Nicholasa Mohr

THE GHOST CHILDREN by Eve Bunting

THE GHOST IN THE BIG BRASS BED by Bruce Coville

HORSE CRAZY (Saddle Club #1) by Bonnie Bryant

THE INCREDIBLE JOURNEY by Sheila Burnford

IRISH RED by Jim Kjelgaard

SEAL CHILD by Sylvia Peck

THE WILD MUSTANG

Joanna Campbell

A BANTAM SKYLARK BOOK®
NEW YORK • TORONTO • LONDON • SYDNEY • AUCKLAND

RL 5, 008-012

THE WILD MUSTANG

A Skylark Book / March 1989

Skylark Books is a registered trademark of Bantam Books, a division of Bantam Doubleday Dell Publishing Group, Inc. Registered in U.S. Patent and Trademark Office and elsewhere.

ISBN 0-553-15698-5

Published simultaneously in the United States and Canada

Bantam Books are published by Bantam Books, a division of Bantam Doubleday Dell Publishing Group, Inc. Its trademark, consisting of the words "Bantam Books" and the portrayal of a rooster, is Registered in U.S. Patent and Trademark Office and in other countries. Marca Registrada. Bantam Books, 1540 Broadway, New York, New York 10036.

PRINTED IN THE UNITED STATES OF AMERICA

OPM   14   13   12   11   10   9   8   7   6

To Suzanne Lammi, fine horsewoman and friend, who appreciates the merits of the mustang.

With my special thanks to Judy Gitenstein and Suzanne Ziegler, two of the nicest editors with whom I've had the opportunity to work.

One

"Come on, Colin." Tracy Jordan banged on her brother's bedroom door. "If you don't hurry up, we won't get up to the meadows in time!"

"Okay! I'm coming," Colin cried.

Tracy tapped her boot impatiently as she waited for her brother to change out of his school clothes. On most days Tracy thought her life on their Wyoming sheep ranch was just about perfect, but that morning, she'd seen Jenks, her father's ranch hand, heading up the mountain road in the Jeep—and that meant trouble for the wild animals who roamed there.

Colin's door finally flew open, and he hurried out, still pulling on his boots. The room behind him was in its usual state of disorder. Clothes were flung on the chair. His books were on the floor. Rock and butterfly collections covered his dresser and desk. His fishing gear was propped in one corner, and his butterfly net in another. "You hardly gave me enough time to change," he said, scowling.

"You're just slow." Tracy was already hurrying down the hall toward the kitchen of the

1

big log ranch house. Colin rushed to keep up. He was only ten to Tracy's twelve, and she'd been growing fast in the last year. She was more than a head taller.

In a few minutes Tracy and Colin had collected their backpacks from the small room behind the kitchen. As they crossed the drive in front of the house, Shag, their pet black-and-white border collie, trotted happily at their heels. The small collies were a valuable asset on the sheep ranch, and Mr. Jordan kept quite a few. The other dogs spent their time with the sheep or in the kennel near the barn, but Shag was the children's special pet. He had his own doghouse behind the house and went everywhere with Tracy and Colin.

The May air was still chilly, and snow covered the peaks of the Grand Tetons in the distance. The ranch was in a small, circular valley. The big barn and ranch house were in the center of the valley, surrounded by sheep pens. Beyond the pens the grazing lands rolled away on all sides and lifted toward the forested mountain slopes.

Tracy set a face pace, but her brother was just as anxious as she was to get there. When Jenks went up the mountain in the Jeep, he set out snares, traps, and poisoned meat for the coyotes, and checked for herds of wild mustangs. If he found any mustangs, he and some ranch hands would go back and capture them. Then the horses would be shipped off to a slaughterhouse.

"Do you think Jenks saw any mustangs this morning?" Colin asked breathlessly.

"I sure hope not," Tracy answered.

"They don't hurt anything."

"Tell Dad that." Tracy made a sour face. "He thinks the mustangs are all mean, useless animals who ruin the grazing lands, but it's the sheep who do that. They eat the grass too close to the roots."

Tracy had never been able to understand her father's stubborn hatred of horses—and mustangs in particular. He wouldn't even allow a horse on the ranch. They were the only family in the area that Tracy knew of that didn't own some horses. He never explained why he felt that way about horses and got angry when Tracy tried to talk to him about it. The most he'd ever say was, "Because of what happened once"—but that didn't explain anything! That was why it was so important for Tracy and Colin to save as many of the mustangs as they could. There were so few still running free.

Brother and sister headed straight up the valley toward the summer grazing lands. Those mountain meadows weren't fenced in by anything except the thick stand of trees surrounding them, and they were a perfect spot for mustangs. If Tracy and Colin saw any, they'd do their best to scare them as far away from the ranch as possible. The land beyond the meadows was national forest, and the mustangs would be protected there.

"We'll probably find some traps today," Colin said after a few minutes of silence.

"If Jenks went up, we will. I just hope we get to them before the coyotes do." Tracy pushed some blond curls off her forehead. The hard walking had made her hotter than she'd thought.

They'd left the flat valley behind and were climbing the first of the hills toward the pine- and beech-covered mountains. Winters in Wyoming were cold, and snow still covered the shady spots under the trees. The last few days had been warm enough to turn the remaining snow to slush, and in the clear spots a few brave plants were pushing up their heads. The mustangs would be looking for that new growth after their limited winter diet.

As Tracy and Colin climbed a rocky path through the pines, Shag bounded ahead of them with his nose to the ground. Every few minutes the dog looked back to make sure they were still in sight. Shag had been trained to herd sheep, but he could sniff out the hidden bits of poisoned meat, and he seemed to know where to find the traps.

The dog suddenly shot off the path and

4

circled some nearby rocks. Tracy and Colin quickly followed. Sure enough, Shag had found a stash of meat. Tracy slipped her backpack off her shoulders. They were always well prepared when they hiked the woods and meadows above the ranch. She took out a dark green plastic bag and a pair of tongs. Then she picked up the meat, dropped it in the bag, and fastened the bag shut. They couldn't bury the meat in the woods where an animal might smell it and dig it up. Instead, they'd bring it back to the ranch and stash it in the shed with the family garbage. No one ever looked in those closed garbage bags.

"One down." Colin gave a whoop.

Shag had bounded off again, and they hurried after him. Not too much farther up the trail, they found a trap. They used a stout fallen branch to trigger it shut. Of course, there was always the chance that Jenks would wonder about all the sprung traps and put two and two together, but they had to take that chance.

A half an hour later, they reached the first of the high, protected meadows. The snow had melted, and the grass was already turning green in the warm sunlight. Climbing to the highest spot in the meadow, they looked around. They were in luck!

At the far side of the meadow, near the trees, a small herd of mustangs was grazing peacefully. The wind was blowing toward Tracy and Colin, and the horses hadn't scented them yet. Tracy sighed in excitement and pleasure. The horses were so beautiful. She'd loved horses as long as she could remember, but because her father hated them, she knew she'd never have one to call her own.

"Do you think Jenks saw them?" Colin asked softly.

"I'll bet he did."

"Which way should we spook them?" Colin was already opening his pack and taking out a coil of rope.

Tracy did the same. "Through the pass toward the mountains," she said. The ranch hands couldn't get through the pass except on foot. It would be too much trouble for them to search for the horses there.

Brother and sister moved down along the edge of the meadow toward the horses. Shag was ready to do his part, too. He'd seen the horses and was waiting for Tracy's signal.

They had to approach from below to get the horses moving in the right direction. When they were a hundred yards away, they uncoiled their ropes, or lariats, and began swinging them above their heads. Tracy signaled to Shag and started the dog moving toward the horses. His eyes never left the mustangs.

When Shag was in position, Tracy and Colin gave whooping yells. The mustangs' heads shot up. The horses immediately reacted. With shrill whinnies and tails high, they spun around and began galloping away from the screaming kids, up the meadow toward the pass. Tracy and Colin followed at a run, swinging their lariats. Tracy turned slightly to the right, and Colin ran to the left to keep the horses from turning off before they reached the pass. Shag completed the maneuver by zigzagging behind the moving animals.

The terrified mustangs surged straight ahead through the break in the trees. They continued on into the narrow pass. Their hooves pounded over the ground and sounded like thunder.

Tracy and Colin were both panting from their hard uphill run when they paused at the top of the pass. The mustangs were still galloping on away from the ranchland.

"Won't Jenks be disappointed!" Tracy chuckled when she'd caught her breath.

Colin recoiled his lariat. "Do you think he knows what we're doing?"

"If he does, he hasn't said anything to Dad yet. And how could he prove it?"

"I don't know, but sometimes I get scared he'll catch us."

"We're doing the right thing, Colin."

"I know!"

Tracy gave a sharp whistle to call Shag. He

came trotting back with his tongue hanging and his tail wagging.

"Good boy!" she told the dog as she patted his head. "We better get going. We'll have just enough time to check the next meadow."

"You think Jenks put some traps over there?"

"He usually does."

The walk downhill was much easier, and within minutes they were at the next meadow. They saw no sign of mustangs, but near the edge of the field, they found a snare—a loop of wire stretched on the ground to catch the foot of an unsuspecting animal.

Tracy shook her head as she snipped the wire into harmless pieces and threw them away. "This is disgusting! I wish Jenks would quit."

"Dad says he's the best worker he's ever had."

"Yeah, I guess he does know sheep. They're all he cares about."

As they were leaving the meadow and entering the woods, Tracy suddenly stopped and grabbed Colin's arm. "What's that noise? Did you hear it?"

Both of them listened. Shag stopped, too. "It sounds like some animal grunting. . . ."

The sound came again. This time they heard a terrified whinny clearly. "It's a horse! It must be hurt!" Tracy cried. "Let's find it." They moved farther into the woods, Shag at their heels, then

8

peered through the leafless branches. The horse grunted again, sounding frightened and in pain. Tracy gave Shag the command to stay, and she and Colin hurried in the direction of the noise. In a tiny clearing they saw him.

The horse was as black as coal, with a white star on his forehead. He didn't look much older than a two-year-old—not fully grown. His eyes rolled as he saw them. He snorted in new terror and tried to back away, but his right foreleg was caught in a length of old fence wire. The wire was wrapped so tightly around his lower leg that it had cut into his skin. The horse's frantic attempts to free himself were making the cut worse.

"Wait, Colin," Tracy whispered. "Just stand still until he knows we don't want to hurt him." Carefully she backed a few feet away. She slowly lowered her backpack and reached inside for one of the apples she'd brought. Her fingers searched for the wire cutters, too. The horse had stopped trying to back away, but he was still frightened. He stood staring at them with head lowered and ears flattened back, breathing hard.

"Get the rope out of your pack," she said quietly to Colin. "I'm going to try to get close enough to give him the apple. You slide the rope around his neck, and I'll cut the wire."

Colin nodded and carefully removed the rope.

9

Very slowly and very quietly they approached the horse. "Easy, boy . . . easy . . . we're not going to hurt you," Tracy crooned. "We're going to set you free."

The colt quivered but stood still. He seemed to sense that these people weren't enemies, but his fear of humans ran deep. He didn't completely trust them.

Step by step, Tracy eased closer. She held the apple on her extended palm. The colt sniffed at the fruit. "It's okay," Tracy murmured. "We're going to help you. That's a boy."

It seemed to take forever before she was near enough to hold the apple under the colt's nose. Tracy knew the risk she was taking. The colt could easily turn on her and bite. His ears flicked up from their flattened position. That was a good sign. She felt his hot breath on her hand and knew he was tempted.

As the colt concentrated on the apple, Colin moved closer. He had his rope ready to toss over the horse's neck. The colt finally succumbed and lipped up the apple. Colin moved quickly and in seconds had the rope in place. The colt jerked and flung up his head, but Colin held him firm and prevented him from backing up and pulling the wire any tighter.

Tracy dropped to her knees and clipped away with her cutters. Two snips and the wire was broken. Her hands moved swiftly to untwist the piece that was around the colt's foreleg. She jumped back with the bloody wire in her hand before the colt could lash out in panic with his front hooves.

The colt suddenly realized that the pressure on his leg was gone. He lifted it gingerly, then hobbled forward a few steps. Colin moved with him, holding onto the rope. But the colt soon came to a trembling halt. He was exhausted by his ordeal. He lifted his injured leg as if it pained him.

Tracy continued to speak to him in a soothing voice.

"Let's get him away from the wire," she said to Colin in a minute. "There's a clear spot near the path." Slowly the two of them coaxed the frightened horse forward. His eyes were still rolling, and he was favoring his foreleg, but he came along. Tracy grabbed the backpacks and removed another apple. When they reached the clearing, she gave it to the colt. The offering reassured him. With Colin holding the horse firm, Tracy knelt down beside his injured leg.

She examined it, careful to stay out of range should he decide to lash out. The wire had rubbed away the hair and dug into the colt's skin. The cut needed cleaning and bandaging.

"What do you think?" Colin asked nervously.

"It's pretty bad." Tracy frowned. "We can't let him go like he is. He's lame, and the cut could get infected."

11

"I wonder how long he'd been caught."

"Probably for quite a while."

"What are we going to do?" Colin asked.

There was a frown on Tracy's brow as she studied the injured animal. "We can't bring him back to the ranch. Dad'll just ship him off. Oh, Colin, he's so beautiful! If only we could keep him—at least until he's better."

"Maybe we could hide him someplace," Colin suggested, although he didn't sound very certain about the idea. "It would only be for a little while. Once he's healed, we'd set him free again."

Tracy thought it over, frowning in concentration. Where would the colt be safe from Jenks's spying eyes and safe from the coyotes, too? The coyotes would single out a lame and injured animal. Suddenly her face cleared and she grinned broadly. "I've got it! Remember that old hermit's cabin up by Silver Brook? There aren't any grazing lands near there, and the ranch hands never go into those woods. We could keep him in the cabin and leave Shag as a guard. Then real early in the morning or after dark we could sneak up food and take care of him. We always go hiking in the woods. Nobody would guess we've got the colt!"

Colin's eyes lit as he caught Tracy's excitement. "And nobody'd miss a couple bales of hay. Let's do it!"

12

Tracy turned to the horse. "We're going to take care of you, boy! You're going to be okay now."

The colt gave a soft nicker as if he understood that he was in good hands.

Two

The trip to the old cabin took much longer than it usually did. Because of the colt's injury, they had to go slowly. The horse was obviously relieved to be free from the wire, but he didn't entirely trust these strangers. He wasn't very comfortable with Shag, either. To him, dog scent was almost the same as coyote scent. But when Shag trotted on ahead, ignoring the horse, the colt accepted him.

Finally they heard the splashing of the brook and saw the cabin under the pines on the bank above it.

Tracy stopped them at the brook, and Colin led the colt out into the cool, clean water. The cold must have felt good on the colt's injured leg, and he immediately lowered his head for a long drink. While he was occupied, Tracy splashed water over the cut and gently cleaned it with a bandana that she'd had in her pack. Fortunately the horse didn't object to her gentle touch. She'd find some clean dressings at home and some antiseptic salve and bring them up that night after dinner. Luckily the wire hadn't been rusted.

When the cut was cleaned to Tracy's satisfaction, she wrapped the bandana around it to keep out any more dirt. They then led the colt up to the cabin. No one had used the cabin in years, and it looked it. The windows were boarded up, and the wide plank door swung open on its hinges. The roof shingles didn't look in very good shape, but there were no visible holes.

While Colin held the colt, Tracy went over to inspect the place. She pushed the door open all the way and cautiously looked inside. Any number of animals might have decided to make the cabin their home. She couldn't see much with only the light from the doorway. She went to one of the front windows and tried the boards. They came off with only a few tugs. The windowpanes behind weren't broken, but they were covered with a thick layer of grime. She rubbed the worst away with her jean jacket sleeve and looked through. Aside from some broken furniture, the cabin was empty.

Feeling braver, she went in through the doorway. Shag hurried in after her and made an inspection of his own. The old floors were covered with a layer of dust, but that could easily be swept away with a broom. A table stood in the center on three legs. Beside it were two broken chairs. In one corner were an old crock and some cooking utensils. Otherwise, the room was bare.

She went back out to report to Colin. He'd been busy fashioning an improvised halter out of his rope.

"Where'd you learn to do that?" Tracy asked in surprise.

"I saw it in one of my cowboy books. Looks okay, doesn't it?"

"It sure does." Tracy gave her brother a pat on the shoulder. "The cabin needs to be swept out, and there's some old furniture I can move. We'll need to get him some bedding, too."

As she spoke, the colt watched her attentively. He'd settled down, but that was probably because he was so worn out. He was still a wild animal, Tracy reminded herself. He wasn't used to people or to being confined.

"There's a patch of grass over there," she added to Colin. "Maybe you can let him graze while I get this cleaned up."

Colin led the colt away. The mustang had certainly never been led around on a halter before, but he followed Colin. He'd seen the grass too.

Tracy worked quickly. It would be dark soon, and they had to be home for dinner. She carried the broken chairs outside and pushed the table into a corner out of the colt's way. She removed the boards from one of the back windows to let in more light. The old crock would be great as a water jug. She washed it and filled it in the

17

brook and put it down on the floor near the window. Next she found some dry leaves and stalks of last year's grass. She carried in a few armloads and scattered them over the floor for bedding. The next day she'd sweep out the cabin and find some better bedding. She'd have to sneak a broom up after dark, but the cabin would do for now. Tracy checked the outside door. It still had an old latch that worked. They'd be able to lock the colt in and keep any predators out.

Satisfied, she hurried out and motioned to Colin. The colt wasn't eager to leave the patch of grass. He wouldn't budge. Tracy used the two remaining apples to coax the colt toward the cabin. She was glad she'd brought so many apples along that day. Getting him to walk through the door was a problem too. He'd never been inside a building. In fact, he'd probably never seen a building. But his hunger finally won out over his fear. He stepped hesitantly inside and looked nervously around. At last he followed Tracy to the spot where she'd laid the apples on the floor. He immediately lowered his head and plucked one up.

"We should take off the rope," Tracy said. "I don't want him to trip on it, but we might have trouble getting another rope on him when we get back."

"Well," Colin suggested, "I can cut off the

long part and leave the halter on him. That would be okay, wouldn't it?"

"Great idea. You do that, and I'll bring in some of that grass for him." She left Shag sitting guard at the door in case the colt decided to bolt. She broke off as much of the short new grass as she could. It wasn't much, but it was better than nothing. Tracy placed the grass in an old frying pan that she'd cleaned and set it in front of the colt.

"I think we should leave Shag here to protect him," she said as she finished. "We can bring them both some food when we come back after dinner."

"What if Dad comes looking for us while we're gone? You know what he'd do if he found out!"

Tracy didn't want to think about that at the moment. "I'll figure out something," she said firmly. Yet the fear added a tingle of excitement to their adventure. Tracy wasn't about to chicken out. The colt needed them.

She stood back to inspect the beautiful black animal, who was eating happily. "You know, Colin, now that we're going to keep him for a little while, maybe we should give him a name."

"Yeah, we should . . . but what?"

"He's so black, with just that white star. How about Whitestar?"

Colin nodded his head eagerly. "I like that! It really fits him."

Tracy spoke to the horse. "Did you hear that, boy? You've got a name now. You're Whitestar."

The colt couldn't understand, but he did lift his head briefly to look in their direction. Tracy thought that was a wonderful start.

"See you later," Tracy said as she and Colin reluctantly left the cabin. "You'll be all right, boy. Shag will guard you until we get back."

They latched the door behind them, and Tracy commanded Shag to stay. He'd been left to watch herds of sheep before, so he understood what was expected. He sprawled down in front of the door and dropped his head onto his paws.

"Let's get going!" Tracy said. The two of them set off at a run.

It was growing dark when they reached the ranch house. The kitchen light was burning, and they could see Emily Ward, their housekeeper, setting the table. Emily was an old family friend who had come to the ranch seven years before when Tracy and Colin's mother had died in an auto accident. She was gray-haired, plump, and kindhearted, and Tracy and Colin thought of her more as an aunt than a housekeeper. They dropped their backpacks behind the shed. Colin stayed behind to dispose of the poisoned meat.

"Hi, Emily, we're back," Tracy called as she entered the kitchen.

Emily looked up and smiled. "Just in time for supper. Where have you two been off to for so long?"

Tracy felt her throat go dry. "Just hiking in the woods."

"You know, Tracy," Emily continued after a moment, "you're almost thirteen. Don't you think it's time you had other friends and took an interest in something besides tramping around the ranch with your brother?"

"Well, there's Jason." Tracy stuttered out the first name that popped into her mind. "He comes over sometimes." Jason Colby lived on the neighboring ranch and was in Tracy's class. He was always following her around and trying to talk to her. She thought he was a pest, but that didn't stop him from coming over to the Jordan ranch.

"You don't have any girlfriends," Emily added. "I remember doing a lot of things with my girlfriends when I was your age."

"I have friends at school," Tracy said quickly, "but they all live so far away, and Colin and I have lots of fun." Tracy cast a glance to her brother, who'd just come in the back door.

"I know you do," Emily said, "and I'm glad that you and your brother get along so well together, but you're growing up. How about

21

having a few of your girlfriends out here for a sleep-over or party?"

"I don't know . . ." Tracy sought for some kind of excuse. She'd need all her time for the colt now.

Her father walked down the hall and into the kitchen at that moment. "Trying to turn my daughter into a social butterfly, Emily?" he asked. He laid a hand on Tracy's shoulder. "I don't see anything wrong with what she's doing. Let her enjoy it."

Of course, if her father knew what she and Colin were up to, he might have something different to say, Tracy thought.

"Kids grow up fast enough," he added.

"Yes, I suppose they do," Emily agreed. "Well, go get washed up, kids, and we'll eat in a minute."

Tracy and Colin took turns in the bathroom, then sat down at the round kitchen table.

Their father sat down a moment later. "You kids have a good afternoon?"

"Fine, Dad," they both said quickly.

"I'm going to need your help tomorrow. I've got a load of feed coming in. I'll need you to help stack it."

Tracy and Colin exchanged a look behind their father's back.

"What about the hands?" Tracy asked.

"They'll be busy moving some of the sheep.

With this warm spell, the snow's melting off faster than I expected."

She and Colin would be lucky if they got an hour to spend with Whitestar. Tracy tried not to let her disappointment show. Emily put the food on the table, and they all started filling their plates.

"Jenks found traces of a bunch of mustangs up near the north pasture," Mr. Jordan said as he dug into his food. "I'll have to send the boys up there to see if we can't catch them."

Tracy knew that particular band of mustangs was now safe—she and Colin had chased it away. But there'd be others. Her face paled, and her food suddenly tasted like chopped cardboard.

"One herd means there'll be more coming in with the spring weather," her father continued.

"Why do you hate the mustangs so much, Dad?" The words were out of her mouth before she could stop herself. "They're not hurting the sheep."

"You leave the ranch managing in my hands. Those horses are nothing but pests. They ruin my pastureland. Besides, they're mean renegades and aren't worth any more than a few pounds of dog food! I'm tired of listening to you romanticizing them. We're running a sheep ranch here."

"But—"

Colin kicked her under the table, and Tracy

said no more. Colin was right—they couldn't make their father suspicious. Luckily for them, he was talking to Emily about other ranch business, and Tracy ate the rest of her meal in silence.

When everyone was finished, their father went on into the living room, where he probably would fall asleep in front of the TV set within an hour. Emily said good-night and went to her own tiny wing of the ranch house. Her daily duties were finished when supper was served. It was Tracy and Colin's job to clear the table and do the dishes. Their conversation was limited to whispers until they went to Tracy's bedroom and closed the door behind them. Their father would think they were doing their homework, but they'd finished it on the forty-minute school-bus ride coming home.

"The hands will be in their cabin by now," Tracy said. "You go and get a half a bale of hay out of the barn. I'll find some ointment and stuff for a bandage. I'll meet you out behind the shed."

"Don't forget Shag's food," Colin said.

"I won't. We'll only have time to feed them, fix Whitestar's leg, and get back. We'll be back here and in bed long before Dad comes to say good-night."

Tracy made sure that her father was in his usual chair in the living room, then she tiptoed into the laundry room. She ripped off a section from a clean old sheet Emily kept in a rag box and took an old blanket out of the linen closet. She filled a brown bag with dry dog food for Shag and grabbed a plastic bowl, then found a jar of ointment in the sheep's medicine cabinet in the barn. Then she met Colin behind the shed. Tracy emptied her pack and stashed the sheeting, blanket, ointment, and dog food inside. Colin picked up the half bale of hay, which was still bound with twine, and the two of them set off. They walked as quickly as they could through the darkened woods. Tracy carried a flashlight and held it on the path in front of them. The walk to the cabin took fifteen minutes, but they were both worried about the time, and the trip seemed to take forever.

Shag bounded out to meet them as they neared the cabin. Tracy shone the light around. The cabin door was still closed. Everything looked fine. Colin dropped the hay with a sigh.

"I'll carry the hay tomorrow," Tracy told him. She hurried up to the cabin door, unlatched it, and slowly pushed it open. She spoke quietly to the horse. "Hi there, boy. It's us. We've got some hay for you." She directed the beam of the flashlight across the floor. The colt had recovered from his exhaustion. He snorted at the sudden light and paced in a small circle. His hooves made hollow echoes on the board floor. "Easy . . . easy," Tracy murmured.

Colin hurried up behind her with the hay.

"Slide it over in front of him," Tracy said. "I think he'll be okay when he sees the food."

Colin used his knife to cut the twine around the bale and pushed the bundle across the floor. The colt backed up as Colin entered, but he soon caught the scent of the hay. As Colin stepped away, the colt hesitantly came over, then tore off a mouthful.

"Whew," Tracy breathed. She let the horse eat for a minute and relax, then she and Colin walked over. "You're going to have to hold him and the light while I work on his cut," she told her brother.

"Okay." Colin took a light grip on the improvised halter. The colt continued eating. Tracy removed the bandage and ointment from her pack and knelt beside the colt's foreleg. Carefully she unwrapped the bandana. The colt was hungry and only gave her a quick, sidelong glance before resuming his meal. Maybe he sensed that they were only trying to help him.

The cut was still clean. Tracy opened the jar of ointment and liberally spread it over the wound. It didn't seem to hurt Whitestar. Next she took the strips of sheeting and carefully wrapped them around his lower foreleg. She tightened the bandage enough so that the colt couldn't work it loose and tied off the ends. *That should do*, she thought.

She rose and, with hands on her hips,

watched as the colt set down his hoof. He didn't seem to be favoring it as much as he had that afternoon. That was a good sign. It meant he hadn't done really serious damage to his leg.

Shag had come into the shed and was watching the colt. He walked over and gave the horse a few tentative sniffs. The colt instantly flattened his ears in warning. He may have decided to put up with the humans who were helping him, but he wasn't ready to make friends with a dog.

Shag understood the colt's warning. His tail drooped as he walked away.

"Don't feel bad, Shag," Tracy said. "He's had a lot to get used to today. He'll make friends with you soon."

The dog cocked his head as if he understood and sat down by the cabin door.

Tracy hated to leave the colt, but she knew they had to get back to the house or get caught. She emptied Shag's food into the plastic dish she'd brought. "I guess we'd better leave Shag outside," she said.

"For tonight," Colin agreed, "until they make friends."

Tracy carried Shag's dish outside and carefully spread the blanket in a dry, protected spot near the front door of the cabin. "He should be all right," she said. "He never sleeps inside anyway, except in winter."

Lastly, Tracy refilled the colt's water dish. Shag could walk down to the brook if he got thirsty. She lightly patted the colt's neck. She knew it was too soon to get friendlier than that. Too much human attention might frighten him again. "Good night, boy. See you tomorrow," she said with a last lingering look at the beautiful young horse. For so long she'd dreamed of having a horse. She'd read every horse novel she could find, but since her father hated horses, she'd never imagined she'd be caring for one. Her father wouldn't even allow her and Colin to go out riding at other ranches. She could hardly believe that they'd been lucky enough to have the colt come into their lives.

She carefully latched the door behind her. "You be good, too, Shag. Stay and watch. We'll be up as soon as it's light."

But as she and Colin hurried down the path, Tracy sighed wearily. "This is going to be harder than I thought, Colin. Boy, am I tired."

"Yeah," Colin yawned. "What time are you going to get up?"

"Four-thirty. Dad and the hands won't be up for another hour. You don't have to come with me. I think I can manage the hay."

Colin didn't argue. He didn't like getting up in the morning—Whitestar or no Whitestar.

Tracy fell asleep almost as soon as she laid

28

her head on her pillow, but her last thoughts were of Whitestar and how incredibly exciting the next days were going to be! Her lips were turned in a smile as she slept.

Three

Tracy fidgeted her way through the school day. She had trouble concentrating on what her teachers were saying. All she could think about was Whitestar. The mustang had been okay that morning, although Tracy had only had time to feed him and check him over quickly before hurrying back home with Shag in tow to get dressed for school. She'd been able to sneak in through her open bedroom window, and no one had even known she was gone.

Tracy hated sneaking, but she didn't know what else she was going to do. She and Colin would never be able to save Whitestar if anyone knew the truth. She'd thought about talking to Emily. Emily was understanding about most things, but she didn't like to interfere in their father's ranch business—and the mustangs were definitely ranch business. Tracy decided that she and Colin had no choice but to keep their secret to themselves.

It was going to be hard. She was already tired, and they still had to help their father after school. Only then could they go up the mountain to Whitestar.

At lunch, Tracy took her tray to Page Mason's table. Page was in Tracy's English class. Tracy didn't know her very well, but she did know that Page had a horse and rode it at some of the 4-H shows. Tracy hoped that Page could give her some information about horse care.

"Okay if I sit here?" Tracy asked the other girl.

Page glanced up and smiled. "Sure. How'd you like that homework assignment?"

"Pretty tough." Tracy sat down and unwrapped her sandwich. "We'll have to do a lot of reading." She hesitated. "I wanted to ask you something. You have a horse, don't you?"

"Yeah—Cindy, my mare."

"I need some advice. What's the best thing to do for a horse with a badly cut leg?"

"I didn't know you had a horse!"

"I don't, but I'm doing a report on horses for one of my classes." Tracy felt horrible about the lie, but she couldn't let it get around school that she was taking care of a horse. It might get back to her father.

Page thought it over. "My mare's never had a bad cut. If she did, I'd get the vet to come over and look at her."

"Oh," Tracy said with disappointment.

"Sorry. Have you looked in the library? There must be some books on horses."

"I'll check. Thanks anyway."

But Page could tell her a lot of other things about horse care, and Tracy listened eagerly as she finished her lunch. She then hurried to the school library and took out every book she could find on horses. She started reading them voraciously during her study hall. She had a lot more to learn, but she was feeling a little more assured about helping Whitestar.

Somehow Tracy found the strength that afternoon to shift the bales of hay from where they'd been unloaded outside the barn. Her father had run out of the hay he'd stored for winter, and there was still a month left before the sheep could graze on fresh grass alone. He also kept several head of cattle, and they had to be fed. The hay had to be stacked high and dry inside, safe from the elements.

Colin had been able to sleep that morning, and he had more energy than Tracy. He lugged two bales to her one, but they were still at work for more than an hour and a half.

"Why don't you go up to the cabin now," he offered when they were nearly finished. "I'll meet you there when I'm done."

Tracy pushed her hair out of her eyes and pulled bits of hay from her curls. "You mean it?

Thanks, Colin! I was really getting tired. Besides, I'm getting worried."

"Yeah, me too. If Dad says anything, I'll tell him you had a nature project, or something."

"You're pretty nice—for a brother."

Colin made a face. "It's only because of Whitestar."

Tracy hurried into the house and grabbed up her backpack. She'd already stashed a bale of hay, an old broom, and a bucket in the woods to be brought up to the colt. None of the items would be missed. All she needed were the medicine and fresh bandages for his leg, and some apples and carrots, too, for treats. She wanted the colt to learn to trust her as soon as possible, though she knew the dangers of turning him into a pet. If Whitestar was to survive in the wild, he couldn't lose all his fear of humans. It was a sad thing for Tracy to think about.

She grabbed a couple of cookies for herself. She was thankful she didn't see Emily before she left the house. She didn't want to have to try to explain why she was running off for the woods before all the hay was stacked. Tracy wolfed down the cookies hungrily as she gathered the hay, the broom, and the bucket and trudged up the mountain. With all she was carrying, she had to stop several times to rest. She'd had to leave Shag at the ranch all day so her father wouldn't notice he was missing, and she was worried. The colt was all alone. Finally she reached the cabin.

Whitestar stomped and snorted when he heard her outside the cabin door. "It's okay, boy. It's just me," she called. She knew the colt must be uncomfortable cooped up in the cabin. She'd brought along a length of rope and had already decided she would walk him for a while. Even with his injured leg, he'd need some exercise.

Tracy eased the door open and called to the colt before stepping inside. "Hello, Whitestar. Sorry to leave you alone for so long. I've got a treat for you . . . and then we'll go for a walk."

The colt pranced uneasily, showing his wild nature and reminding Tracy that he *was* a mustang. But he was beginning to know the sound of her voice. He didn't shy away, but he stood and watched her warily. Tracy closed the door behind her for safety and walked toward him. "Here, look what I've got."

The colt sniffed and gradually let her get close. A second later he took the carrot she offered. Tracy saw that the hay they'd left was gone. She saw, too, that she'd have to clean out his temporary stable. The bedding was littered with droppings.

She tied the end of the rope to his halter— her brother had done a good job—and when Whitestar was done eating, she gently tugged on the rope and started walking toward the door. It wouldn't have been smart to force Whitestar to come, but he seemed eager to leave the cabin. He stepped forward willingly and waited as Tracy pulled open the door. She kept a tight grip on her lead rope as she let him look outside. His ears shot forward, and he whiffed the fresh air with excitement.

"We're going for a walk, boy."

The colt tried to bolt ahead of her through the doorway. There wasn't room for both of them to go through at the same time. She held him firmly and squeezed through first, then let him walk out.

He lifted his head and pranced in a half circle around Tracy.

"It's good to be outside, isn't it?" Tracy laughed. "Come on, we'll walk up here where there's some grass." As she led him forward, she studied his injured leg. He didn't seem to be limping or favoring it, and she breathed a sigh of relief. She'd been so afraid the injury was much worse than she could handle—and then what would she have done?

The colt didn't seem terribly interested in the grass. He was too excited by the outdoors. Tracy led him around the small clearing, then up into the woods where the trees weren't too overgrown. He kept trying to go faster than a walk. Tracy was tempted to let him have his way and to jog along beside him, yet she knew that the faster, more jarring pace wouldn't be good for his foreleg. They both had to be patient. She held him to a slow pace, but walked him farther and longer than she'd originally intended.

As they walked, the colt showed his natural curiosity and intelligence. He held his head high and turned to look everywhere. But he was still nervous, and shied at the smallest rustlings in the bushes as bustling squirrels and birds hunted for nest-building materials. He didn't want to stray off the path, either. He probably associated the thicker woods with the wire that had trapped him.

But Tracy was happy with the progress they'd made. He was allowing her to lead him. He wasn't fighting her or trying to break away, and soon he would get over his other fears. She hated to bring their walk to an end, but she finally led the colt back down the path to the stream. She tied him there and went for her ointment and bandages.

Very carefully she removed the old sheeting, and saw something that made her heart stop—fresh blood. The wound had opened with all the exercise. She should have been more careful! She probably shouldn't have walked him at all. But he still wasn't limping. Maybe that was a good sign. If only she knew more about taking care of horses! If her father hadn't hated them so much, she probably would have had a horse of her own. Most of the kids at school who lived outside of town had horses.

But she couldn't worry about that now. It was more important to tend to Whitestar. She examined his leg. She didn't see any signs of dirt or swelling. The cut still seemed clean and uninfected.

First she washed the wound again in the fresh stream waters that came straight from the mountaintop. She applied more ointment, and after she'd led him away from the brook, she wrapped a new bandage around his lower leg.

The colt had taken a long drink, so she let him graze in the grassy clearing. She tied him so that he wouldn't tangle his legs in the rope. Then she grabbed her broom and started sweeping out the cabin floor and brushing the cobwebs from the ceiling. Boy, was it dirty! She was sneezing by the time she got done. The place looked much better, but the cabin needed more fresh air. She was tugging away at one of the old windows, which opened from the top, when Colin came huffing up the trail with Shag.

Whitestar had looked up from his grazing when he'd heard Colin and the dog, and now he watched them both with the cautious, wild instincts bred into him. He backed nervously away as Shag trotted straight toward him. But

Shag did something the colt didn't expect. He stopped six feet away from the colt, wagged his tail, and lay down on the grass like a black-and-white ball of fur.

The colt was so surprised by the dog's docile behavior that he took a tentative step forward. Then another . . . and another . . . until he was within touching distance. He lowered his finely shaped head and sniffed the dog. Shag looked at the horse lazily with big brown eyes. He was still panting from the run up the trail and Tracy thought he looked like he was grinning.

Tracy and Colin hid their chuckles as the colt gave the dog another tentative touch. Shag didn't move, except to thump his tail gently. The colt snorted, nodded his head, gave the dog one more long, hard look, then started cropping the grass a few feet away.

"Looks like they're making friends!" Tracy said, smiling.

"Shag knows how to make friends with everybody." Colin beamed with pride. Shag was his special pet. He'd been the one who had selected Shag from the regular sheep dogs when their father had said they could have one dog to keep around the house.

"Well, as long as they're making friends," Tracy said, "can you come and help me? I'm trying to get this window open, and I need to get some more bedding, get Whitestar water, put down his hay, and feed Shag."

"I already fed Shag before we left," Colin answered with a trace of pride.

"That's great, but there's still a *lot* more to do!" Tracy snapped, suddenly feeling very tired.

"See if I'm going to help you anymore," Colin said angrily. "I finished stacking the hay—"

"I'm sorry." Tracy immediately relented, but her brother wasn't finished.

"—*and* I made up a story for you!"

"You did? Who to?"

"Dad. He came by just when I'd finished. He thought you hadn't helped. I told him you had, but you'd just gone inside to the bathroom. He said we'd done a good job." Colin grinned mischievously. "Guess what he gave me?"

Tracy shook her head. "I don't know."

Colin pulled eight one-dollar bills from his pocket and waved them in front of his sister. "Extra—on top of my allowance!" He looked down at his feet, then admitted, "Oh, half's for you."

Tracy took her four dollars with a grin. "Thanks, Colin. Did Dad go into the house?"

"No. He had some other stuff to do and went back to his office."

"Whew," Tracy sighed. She was so afraid of getting caught.

"Well, you said you wanted to work," Colin said, suddenly taking the upper hand. "Let's go."

Tracy laughed. "Yeah, let's. You try and unstick the window. I'll do the bedding and hay."

They finished up half an hour later. Tracy stood back and inspected her work with satisfaction. Whitestar now had a clean, comfortable place to stay. They wouldn't have to come back that night since the colt had plenty of food, but one of them would still have to come up in the morning before school.

Before Tracy untied the horse, she ran her hand over his sleek coat, then up his neck. He permitted her gentle touch without flinching, and he followed her into the cabin without too much protest. Once they were inside, she gave him another carrot as a reward. She grinned from ear to ear when he nickered his thanks.

"See you tomorrow," she said softly with her hand still on his shoulder. "We'll leave Shag inside with you tonight, so you'll have some company."

Colin was already laying Shag's blanket inside the door and placing his bowl of water beside it. "He'll be okay," Colin said as Shag settled down. "I think they're friends now."

"Yeah, so do I." Tracy nodded. "And I'm

glad Shag will be inside tonight. Bye, boy. Keep a good watch." She ruffled the dog's fur.

Colin gave the dog a biscuit and a final pat. With both the dog and horse chewing contentedly, Tracy and Colin left the cabin and carefully latched the door behind them.

"It won't be so bad tomorrow," Tracy said, gathering up her pack.

"Don't forget, I'm going up in the morning for you."

"You're going to wake up that early?"

"I think we should take turns."

Tracy was quiet for a while as they started down the path. Her blond eyebrows drew together over her eyes in concentration. "What do you think of him, Colin?"

"He's sure pretty."

"And he'll probably get even prettier when he gets bigger. You know what I wish?" She sighed.

"What?"

"That I could keep him for my very own horse."

"You can't do that, Tracy!" Colin swung his head around to stare at her. "Dad would *never* let you."

"I know," Tracy said sadly. "We can only keep him until his leg heals and he can go back to the wild. But it's nice to dream about. Think of all the fun we could have."

"Yeah . . ." Colin's voice had grown wistful too.

"At least we know we saved him." Tracy tried to be cheerful. "And he's going to grow up to be a beautiful stallion."

"You betcha!"

Again Tracy sighed. If only Whitestar were hers to keep, and if only her father didn't hate mustangs anymore, how wonderful everything would be!

Four

Tracy was sure that her secret was written all over her face, but her father didn't seem to notice that anything was different in the next two weeks. He was busy with the sheep, and Emily was in the middle of her spring cleaning and said nothing else about friends coming over. Tracy and Colin took turns feeding Whitestar in the mornings. No one had noticed either of them slipping out of the house at dawn, and they could go off on their own in the afternoon without being questioned—as long as they finished their chores first. It was a tiring schedule, but Tracy never complained. It was worth it to see the improvement in Whitestar.

The late May days were becoming longer and sunnier, and the colt seemed to be growing and filling out more with every passing day. He had gradually lost his fear of them and was responding to their love and care. His blue-black coat gleamed in the sun. His long mane and tail were like silk. His head was finely formed and more elegant than most mustangs'. His legs were long. When he was full-grown, he'd stand about six-

teen hands—big for a mustang. Tracy wondered
if there were traces of Thoroughbred in his breed-
ing. Perhaps a Thoroughbred mare or stallion
had gotten loose to breed with the wild herds.
He looked like a shining black shadow as he
moved gracefully back and forth—except for the
single white mark between his eyes.

Tracy knew as she watched him that a bond
was forming between the two of them. She loved
the wild colt, and it was going to break her
heart when she had to set him free.

As if reading her thoughts, Whitestar lifted
his head and walked toward her. Gently he
nudged her with his muzzle and nickered. He'd
never done that before, and Tracy was so happy,
she wanted to cry.

Emily picked Tracy and Colin up at school
on Friday, and the three of them went into town
for the weekly shopping. As Emily took care of
her errands, the kids made a few secret purchases. They went to the big feed store that had
a saddlery attached. Tracy gazed longingly at
the beautifully tooled show saddles with silver
decorating their horns and cantles. In the end
she bought two brushes and a hoof-pick and hid
her purchases in her backpack.

As soon as they got home, Tracy hurried up
through the woods with her backpack, anxious
to try her new brushes. Colin would follow her

up in a little while, since it was his job to help Emily unpack the groceries.

Halfway to the cabin, Tracy suddenly paused for a second, thinking she'd heard a noise. It sounded like something moving through the bushes. She listened intently. She immediately thought of one of the ranch hands, but all of them were busy tending the sheep. She didn't hear the noise again. It must have been a squirrel or bird, she decided. She was getting too jumpy. She continued on to the cabin.

Whitestar did a little dance of pleasure when he saw her, nickering and pushing his nose against her shoulder affectionately. She laughed in happiness. "I'm glad to see you too, boy!"

She led the horse outside to the clearing. His cut was healing. A heavy scab had formed to protect the wound, so she decided to remove the bandage. Then she let him graze as she groomed him with her new brushes. The colt seemed to like the attention, and every so often his muscles rippled in pleasure. The brushing brought out new highlights in his coat. It gleamed like black satin.

"So *that's* what you've been doing!" a voice said from behind her.

Tracy nearly jumped out of her skin. She spun around, feeling the blood drain from her face. Staring back at her in open curiosity was Jason Colby.

"What are *you* doing here?" she barked rudely.

Jason grinned, not the least bit offended. "I followed you. I thought you and Colin were up to something when he never asked me to come over anymore. I rode over after school to see if I could figure out what—and I *did*!"

"Rode?"

"My pony's back in the woods."

"So it was *you* I heard. Well, you can just get lost, Jason!"

"Oh, yeah?" He stuck his hands in his pockets and grinned at her lazily.

Tracy felt a twinge of fear. What if he told someone about Whitestar? She licked her lips and tried to think fast. If she made him angry, he would tell. She smiled at him sweetly, which was something she hardly ever did. Most of the time, she just tolerated him.

"Well . . . now that you're here, I suppose you can stay," she added on a friendlier note.

Jason needed no more encouragement. He hurried over. "Where did you get him?" he asked excitedly. "I thought your dad hated horses."

"He's a mustang. Colin and I found him with his leg caught in some wire. He must have gotten separated from his herd. We cut him free, and we've been letting his leg heal. But if my dad or Jenks ever found out. . . . You won't tell, will you, Jason?"

Jason pretended he was thinking it over, but he was so glad to have Tracy show some sign of friendliness that he didn't hesitate too long. He soon shook his head. "Naw, I won't tell—not if you let me come up here with you."

"We're going to have to set him free pretty soon," Tracy said sadly.

"Why?"

Quickly Tracy told Jason how hard it was to feed and care for the colt without being seen.

As she finished talking, Colin ran into the clearing, out of breath. "Whose horse is that on the path?" he burst out. "What's happened—" He stopped in his tracks when he saw Jason. "Oh, it's only you. I thought someone else had found Whitestar. But how come you're here?"

"I followed your sister. I knew you guys had some kind of secret."

"It's okay," Colin said to his sister. "I'm sure we can count on Jason to keep quiet."

Tracy gave Jason a genuine smile of relief as he nodded.

Jason lifted his snub nose in the air confidently. "I might even help you."

"How?" Tracy asked.

"You know my father keeps lots of horses." Jason's father ran a cattle ranch that bordered the Jordan ranch. The two places were separated by a natural divider of steep hills and woodland. "I could probably get some stuff for you—like a bridle and a blanket, and maybe a saddle."

Tracy's eyes widened. She'd forced herself to be content with making the horse her friend. She hadn't dared think about ever having a chance to ride him.

"And I know something about horses," Jason continued. "I could show you how to do a lot of things."

"You could?" Colin exclaimed.

Tracy was excited, too, but her common sense told her that she'd be foolish to get her hopes up. "There's no way we can keep him. Our father would never let us have a horse at the ranch, and we couldn't leave him up here all year long. I don't even know if he's old enough to ride. He's not full-grown."

Jason went over and examined the horse more closely. He ran his hands over Whitestar's coat and felt his legs. He seemed to know what he was doing. But the colt didn't recognize this stranger's scent and shied away when Jason tried to look in his mouth.

"I could tell how old he is for sure by his teeth," Jason said.

Tracy went to the colt. "Don't force him. He doesn't know you. Besides, he can't be more than two. He's grown since we've had him."

"He's awful pretty for a mustang. Maybe it's because you've been grooming him. My dad could tell you more, just by looking at him."

"You're not going to tell your dad!" Tracy shot back.

"He'd be on your side. He doesn't like what your father does with the mustangs he finds on your land," Jason said firmly. "But you're right—he might say something to your father if I told him. Parents do dumb things sometimes."

Tracy and Colin both nodded. Then Tracy grinned mischievously at Jason. "Well, if you really want to help us, the cabin's got to be mucked out. You can do that."

Jason made a face. "Boy, thanks a lot," he said, but he headed toward the cabin anyway. This was the most attention Tracy'd ever shown him. He thought she was the cutest girl in their class, even if she did wear braces, and the most fun, too. She didn't go around giggling and doing silly things like most of the girls.

"I'll help you," Colin offered, following. Jason had always been his friend, and Colin looked up to the older boy with a bit of hero worship.

When all the work was finished in half the time it normally took, Jason suggested that he get Dusty, his pony, and see if he and Whitestar would make friends.

Tracy shook her head. "Whitestar will really hate being left alone if he gets friendly with another horse. . . ."

"Yeah, I suppose you're right. Maybe in a couple of days."

Tracy put Whitestar in the cabin and left Shag with the horse She gave the colt her usual good-bye caresses. He didn't seem to want her to go, and she didn't want to leave him either. It was getting harder every time she said good-bye.

The three kids started down the trail, and Jason collected his pony from where he'd tethered him under a tree. He led him along behind as they headed toward the ranch and talked about their plans for the colt. No one would think anything of seeing Jason at the ranch.

"I've been thinking," he said quietly before mounting up. "You need some better bedding. My father uses sawdust. Dusty and I can bring over a bag tomorrow."

"Do you think your father would miss it?" Tracy asked. "I don't want you to get into trouble because of me."

Jason's cheeks turned red. "He won't miss it—besides, it's real cheap."

"I can pay you," Tracy offered. It was one thing to sneak hay from their own ranch, but she didn't like Jason taking his father's supplies.

Jason shook his head. "Dad would probably tell me to take it if he knew we were trying to save a horse. See you tomorrow. I'll come up as soon as my chores are done."

They waved good-bye to their fellow conspirator and went in to wash up for dinner.

Emily smiled as they came into the kitchen. "I'm glad to see that Jason came by. He hasn't been here in a while. I thought maybe you'd had an argument."

"No," Tracy said quickly. "He's just been busy."

"You'll get to see more of each other now that summer's almost here." Emily gave Tracy a sly grin.

"Oh, Emily—*please!*" Tracy felt her face flush. She was relieved to escape to the bathroom when Emily told her to wash up for dinner.

Five

With all the hours they were spending with Whitestar, Tracy and Colin had had to abandon their search for traps and poisoned meat. It bothered both of them, but the hands were so busy with the sheep and new lambs that they worked from dawn until dark. Tracy and Colin could only hope that Jenks hadn't had time to set out new traps. Still, Tracy's biggest concern was Whitestar. She knew her days with the colt were numbered, and she wanted to spend every minute she could with him before she returned him to the wild.

She was thinking of the colt and her plans for the afternoon when she and Colin came up the drive from the school bus. As they passed the barn, they saw the Jeep parked in front. That wasn't unusual, but when they glanced inside the Jeep, Tracy let out a horrified cry. A dead coyote was draped across the back seat.

Tracy felt like she was going to get sick. She covered her eyes with her hand and spun away. Colin turned away, too, with his head hanging.

Jenks had come out of the barn in time to

see their reactions. "What's the matter with you two?" he asked. "These coyotes aren't worth nothing. All they do is kill the sheep. About time I caught a couple."

"I think it's disgusting!" Tracy gasped.

Jenks chuckled. "You'd think you two had been brought up in the city instead of on a ranch." He paused, then spoke in a sly voice. "Funny, but I've been finding an awful lot of my traps sprung."

All Tracy could do was shake her head and run for the house before she started to cry. She dashed down the hall to her room. Colin was right behind.

"It's not our fault, Tracy," he whispered. "We couldn't take care of Whitestar and check for traps, too."

"I know, but I just feel so awful. That poor coyote. He didn't do anything wrong. Nobody's reported any dead sheep."

Colin nodded, his eyes wet with tears.

Emily came into the room a minute later and sat down on the edge of the bed. "I saw what happened," she said gently. "I'm sorry you kids had to see that. I know how you love animals."

"But, Emily, why do they have to kill them?" Tracy groaned.

"It's a sad fact of life on a ranch. Your father has to work real hard to make the ranch pay for itself. The loss of even a few spring lambs can make a big difference." She laid a hand on both of their shoulders. "But I know how you feel. I wish it didn't have to be this way either."

That night at dinner, Tracy screwed up her courage and tried to talk to her father about the coyotes. He listened to her arguments, but he had the same opinions as Jenks. All he cared about were his sheep and their safety. "Would you feel any better if Jenks had to bring down a couple of dead lambs?" he asked.

Tracy wagged her head and lowered her eyes. "No, I'd feel just as bad."

"Well, there you are. It's either the coyotes or the sheep," he said firmly.

Tracy knew it was useless to argue. No one had found any dead sheep, but her father would only tell her that that was because they'd gotten rid of the coyotes.

"At least we haven't seen any sign of mustangs," he added with satisfaction. "Maybe we cleaned out the worst of them last year."

Her father had no idea how those words hurt Tracy. She'd never have the courage to tell him just how much she loved those horses— and one in particular. She sat silently through the rest of the meal, more worried than ever about Whitestar. And now Jenks was suspicious of her and Colin. He'd noticed the sprung traps.

He didn't have proof that they'd done it, but he just might watch them from now on.

That night she decided to bring Shag back down to the ranch with her. Jenks's suspicions had made her uneasy. There was no point in asking for trouble, and sooner or later, someone would notice that the dog wasn't sleeping in his doghouse behind the ranch house. Shag was glad to be home, but Tracy worried over the colt. It was his first night alone, and he'd gotten used to Shag's company. She'd spent extra time grooming and walking him that afternoon and had double-checked the latch on the cabin door to be sure he'd be safe.

Still, she went up earlier than usual the next morning. When she opened the cabin door, her heart started hammering in panic. The shed was a mess. Whitestar's water bucket was turned over and battered. The walls of the cabin were scarred from flying, pounding hooves. The colt had obviously been desperately trying to escape.

He stood nervously quivering, then made a dash for the open door. Tracy managed to close it before he bolted out. She grabbed the colt's halter, not thinking of her own safety, and tried to soothe him with words and gentle hands. All the while her thoughts were racing. What had happened to scare him so? Had he simply gotten mad at being left alone? She quickly tied a lead rope to his halter. She kept a firm grip on the rope as she eased open the door and started leading him outside.

His ears shot forward, and his eyes rolled as he scented the air. He made a noise somewhere between a cry and a whinny, a sound full of fear.

"It's all right, Whitestar," Tracy said soothingly. "Nothing's going to happen to you while I'm here. And see, I've brought Shag."

The colt wasn't reassured. Neither was Tracy when she saw Shag frantically nosing around outside the cabin. Every so often he gave a low, menacing growl from deep in his throat. Shag paused by a spot underneath the front window, and Tracy led the protesting colt a few steps forward to get a better look.

Her stomach tightened. The evidence was clear. The dirt beneath the window was marked by paw prints—and they weren't Shag's. The logs of the cabin wall bore long scratch marks. Coyotes or wolves, and they'd been trying to get to Whitestar through the partially opened window. The open part of the window was too high up for them to reach, but their efforts must have terrified Whitestar. As upset as Tracy was, she couldn't hate the coyotes for what they'd done. They were only following their instincts. If Whitestar hadn't been hurt and had been running free, they wouldn't have gone after him.

"You poor baby." Tracy laid her cheek against the colt's sleek neck. "You must have been so scared! And nobody was here to help you!" She could feel the colt's muscles quivering and quickly led him away from the coyote scent to the clearing behind the cabin. "I won't leave you alone again," she said anxiously. "I promise!"

The colt restlessly stomped his uninjured foreleg, pawing the earth. He wanted to put some distance between himself and the cabin. Yet, because of the growing bond of trust between the girl and the horse, he slowly quieted. Tracy walked him and let him graze until he seemed to have put his nighttime visitors out of his mind. Then she tied him and brushed away the coyote sign with a pine branch. She didn't know if that would do any good, but she felt she had to do something.

The colt didn't want to go back into the cabin. Tracy could understand his fear. She tried to coax him through the doorway, but he stood with hooves planted firmly and refused to budge until Shag went through the doorway before him. The dog's presence seemed to reassure him, but Tracy knew she'd have to get up to the cabin as soon as she could after school. Otherwise the colt would panic again.

She was going to be late getting back, but that couldn't be helped. She only hoped Emily hadn't come to her room to make sure she was up. Tracy felt like crying in frustration as she ran down the trail to the ranch. From the hillside above the ranch, she saw the ranch hands moving around the bunkhouse and barn, getting ready to start their day. Carefully, she slipped from tree to tree, using them as cover until she was a few yards from the back of the house. Suddenly the kitchen door opened, and Emily stepped out with a bag of trash. She started toward the shed and saw Tracy.

Tracy knew there was no point in trying to hide. She stood up a little straighter and tried to look innocent.

"What are you doing out so early?" Emily asked. "I thought you were still in the shower."

"Uh . . . well, I woke up real early and couldn't go back to sleep. I decided to take a walk." That wasn't really a lie, Tracy thought. She had gotten up early, and she had taken a walk.

Emily accepted the explanation without question. "Well, come on in. Breakfast's ready."

Tracy and Colin had a conference on the school bus that morning.

"Boy," Colin said, wide-eyed, "I was sure you were gonna get caught. How come you were so late?"

Tracy explained about the coyotes.

"Uh oh, that's bad," Colin said. "You shouldn't have brought Shag down last night."

"I was afraid someone would notice he was gone," Tracy said miserably. All the sneaking was bothering her conscience. If only their father didn't hate mustangs. If only she and Colin could confide in him and have him understand.

"What are we going to do now?" Colin asked.

Tracy shook her head. "I left Shag at the cabin. We'll have to leave him up there every night and take our chances that no one will notice."

"Whitestar's almost healed, isn't he?" Colin seemed reluctant to bring up the question.

"Yeah," Tracy said slowly. "There's only a little scab left."

"We could let him go."

Tracy nodded and sighed. She knew that was an answer, but she couldn't stand to think about it. She loved Whitestar. If she let him go, she'd never see him again. Her whole life would seem so empty. She didn't know how she'd gotten along before without the excitement of the colt.

Colin didn't say anything more. He wanted to keep the colt as much as she did.

"We'll figure out something," Tracy said with more confidence than she felt.

Six

Tracy tried to put her worries and doubts out of her mind and think only about the positive. Jason's help did make a difference. Whitestar liked his new bedding, and it was much easier to clean out the cabin now. Tracy took the precaution of carrying the dirty bedding away from the cabin and dumping it in the woods. Horse droppings around the cabin would immediately draw suspicion if anyone passed by.

The colt was growing happier and more at ease with his new friends. He whinnied when he heard them coming and rubbed his head against each of them in turn. But Tracy was his favorite. His animal instincts seemed to tell him that she'd saved his life.

Tracy had to admit that Jason wasn't such a pain after all. The things he brought over for Whitestar were great. He supplied a real halter—an old one that his father didn't need, but it was more comfortable for Whitestar than the rough rope. He brought over a lead rope, too, that clipped onto the halter and made it easier to tie and untie the colt. He'd found an old bridle, but they'd all decided that Whitestar wasn't ready for that step yet.

Tracy took care of most of the colt's exercise, running him around in wide circles in the meadow up the hill. Jason and Colin would sit and watch, and Jason would make appreciative comments and suggestions.

"Make believe there's a couple of barrels in the field," he called to Tracy. "Run him around them. Yeah, like that," he added when she followed his instructions. "Bet he could turn on a dime. Boy, would I like to train him for the barrel race!"

Tracy wanted to see how Whitestar looked for herself. It was hard to judge when she was running next to him. She gave Jason the lead line and had him run the colt around. She grinned broadly as she studied the two of them. At a jog, or trot, the colt moved with a sleek, smooth grace. She could imagine how he would perform at a quicker pace like a canter, but none of them would be able to run fast enough to keep up with him at that speed.

Her eyes were glowing when Jason walked the colt back to the side of the meadow. She threw her arms around Whitestar's neck and sighed happily. "You're wonderful, Whitestar . . . the best horse in all of Wyoming."

"When he's full-grown and gets some training," Jason agreed enthusiastically, "he just might be."

Yet Tracy knew that would never happen. The day would never come when she could keep Whitestar and train him—not if her father had anything to say about it.

A few days later Tracy went up to tend the colt alone. Colin was going to wait for Jason before coming to the cabin. The colt was as happy as ever to see Tracy, and just being with Whitestar made her feel better. She groomed him and let him graze as she cleaned out the cabin and threw down some fresh sawdust. Then she led Whitestar up the hill toward the higher meadow behind the cabin.

The meadow was large, but since it was surrounded by woodland and hard to get to, it was never used by the ranch for the sheep. She and Whitestar left the woods and mounted a rise. There was a flat area on the other side where she usually exercised the colt.

A small band of mustangs was grazing on the far side where the mountain forest sloped down to the meadow. The wild horses were of varying colors, from dark bay to buckskin to black-and-white pinto. There were about a dozen, and Tracy noticed a stallion and several mares with young foals at their sides. They looked so peaceful and content and were such a beautiful sight to Tracy that she didn't stop to think of Whitestar's reaction until it was too late.

Whitestar lifted his head with a jerk. Tracy gripped the lead more firmly as the colt's ears shot forward, and his finely shaped nostrils flared wide as he sniffed the air. He made some soft, excited noises and strained against the lead rope.

Suddenly the stallion sensed Whitestar's presence. He lifted his own head and stared intently in their direction. He was a big and battle-worn palomino. His neck was arched, and his mane and tail flowed proudly as he trotted several yards from the mares for a better view of the intruders. His nose was up, scenting the air.

Whitestar gave a resounding whinny. That was all the stallion needed to hear. He was instantly alert. He pranced in a small circle, then struck the earth with one forefoot. Suddenly Tracy realized the possible danger to both of them. Whitestar was a male too, and he was intruding in this stallion's territory. The stallion might want to fight!

The stallion looked both magnificent and threatening. Tracy swallowed hard and took a firmer grip on Whitestar. The colt trembled and whoofed excited breaths through his nose. He danced sideways, and Tracy jumped out of the way of his hooves. The colt wasn't thinking of her now. He was thinking about the stallion and the mares.

The stallion gave a high, piercing cry. It sounded to Tracy like a challenge . . . or a warning. Whitestar answered. In that instant he forgot his contact with humans. He yearned to be with his own kind.

The mares had all lifted their heads and were ready to make a mad dash away on the stallion's signal, but he only gave them a quick look over his shoulder. His attention was concentrated on Whitestar. The stallion paced back and forth like a powerful athlete, with his head turned in Whitestar's direction.

With excited whinnies, Whitestar surged against the lead line in an effort to go forward. Tracy held him with both hands. Her palms were growing sore from holding so tightly to the lead rope. She needed every ounce of strength to keep the colt from bolting.

Even as she struggled with him, she knew that this was the moment she'd been dreading. Whitestar was fully healed. He was healthy and fit. She could give the colt his freedom and let him go off to the herd. All she had to do was unclip the lead, and Whitestar would pound off without a backward look.

She couldn't do it! Her hands refused to move. Tears filled her eyes as she battled with herself. She had no right to keep the colt. She couldn't offer him a home—and someday again soon she would be forced to make the same decision she was fighting against now.

Yet Tracy also knew the dangers in releasing Whitestar to deal with the old stallion's challenge. She wasn't just making excuses for keeping the colt. Whitestar was a stallion as well, though a very young one. The old warrior stallion wouldn't allow him to join the herd. He'd fight or try to drive Whitestar away. Whitestar was young and inexperienced. He might be injured. Tracy couldn't stand the thought of it. One day Whitestar would fight for his own herd of mares, but Tracy knew he'd never win the battle now.

The old stallion circled closer, curious and confused by this adversary who didn't come to meet him and didn't retreat either. Whitestar had a will of his own and he was very strong. Tracy couldn't pull him back into the woods. She couldn't even cry out to the stallion and frighten him away with the sound of her voice. In her panic, her cries died in her throat. She couldn't make a sound.

The old stallion had caught her scent. He stopped and snorted uneasily. But when Whitestar let out another piercing cry, the stallion forgot his fear and started circling forward again. He was enraged and ready for battle.

Tracy knew she would soon have no choice but to let Whitestar go. She might be trampled if she didn't. If the stallion overcame his fear of her scent, nothing would stop him, and the two horses would fight.

She didn't hear the voices and footsteps behind her until Jason and Colin had reached her side. Both boys stared at the scene before them with wide eyes.

"Oh, wow!" Colin exclaimed under his breath.

"I don't believe this," Jason added.

Tracy finally found her voice, but it came out in a harsh, barely audible rasp. "Don't just stand there—*do* something! Scare him away . . . anything!" She couldn't hold on to the lead rope much longer. Her hands were rubbed raw and her arms ached. And Whitestar was struggling harder than ever. He tried to rear up. It was all Tracy could do to hold him and avoid his flailing hooves.

The boys finally acted. Screaming at the tops of their lungs, they ran forward waving their arms. Although they stopped well away from the old stallion, their antics were too much for him. He spun in his tracks and, with his tail waving high like a golden flag, he pounded off to his mares. The mares needed no further encouragement to pick up their own heels and surge off through a gap in the trees, departing in a cloud of dust.

The old stallion paused before he entered the woods. Silhouetted in the sunlight, he reared, and his front legs slashed the air. Then he gave a last echoing cry, and galloped away.

Whitestar answered the cry and lunged against the lead rope. Jason ran back to help Tracy. He slid his fingers through the opposite side of the halter and held the colt's head. Colin took the lead rope from Tracy. After clinging to the rope for so long and so hard, she could barely open her fingers.

The colt was sweating and stomping his hooves in his excitement. It took all of Tracy, Colin, and Jason's coaxing to quiet him, then many minutes to get him to turn and start back through the woods. He wouldn't move faster than a slow walk and kept trying to crane his head around to look over his shoulder.

Tracy felt shaken. Her legs didn't seem to want to support her. "Boy, am I glad you guys came when you did," she said weakly as they walked back to the cabin.

"Lucky timing," Colin said. "How long were you up there?"

Tracy shook her head. "I don't know. It seemed like forever. I almost let him go, Colin. I thought maybe this was his chance to be free again. But then the old stallion started acting funny, and I knew they'd fight if I let Whitestar loose. I—I couldn't do it." She choked back a sob.

"It's okay," Jason said. "I couldn't have done it either."

Colin nodded in agreement.

When they got to the cabin, they led the colt over to the tiny clearing behind the cabin and tied him, and Tracy collapsed cross-legged on the ground.

"I guess we can't bring him up to the meadow anymore," she said, "until we check first."

"Do you think the stallion will come back?" Colin asked worriedly.

"I don't think so," Jason answered. "We scared him pretty good, and he'd never come as far as the cabin."

"I hope not." Tracy exhaled sharply. She suddenly looked around. "Where's Shag?"

"I left him home," Colin said. "Dad came by the house when we were leaving and said something about Shag not being around much lately."

"He'll probably think it's even stranger that you left Shag home. He goes everywhere with us."

Colin gave an exasperated sigh. "I can't think of everything, Tracy!"

"Sorry, I guess that run-in with that old stallion really scared me. And it just seems to get harder and harder to keep everything secret."

Jason and Colin dropped to the ground be-

71

side her, and Jason put a friendly arm around her shoulders. "Don't worry, Tracy. Now that you've got both of us to help you, I'm sure we'll be able to think of something."

Seven

In mid-June school was dismissed for the summer. Tracy, Colin, and Jason couldn't have been happier. Things would be much easier for them during vacation. They had their summer chores to do, but they were still left with the long afternoons to themselves. With more time on their hands, the job of tending to Whitestar was simpler. They didn't have to sneak up to the cabin so early in the morning or so late at night.

But Tracy was still nervous. Jenks hadn't said anything else to them, but she didn't trust him. Fortunately, he and the other hands were so busy moving the sheep that Tracy and Colin didn't see much of him.

The colt was growing more and more beautiful, and more and more trusting of his three human friends—and Shag, too. He seemed to have forgotten the stallion and the herd of mustangs, but Jason had introduced Dusty to the colt, so Whitestar had another horse to keep him company during the afternoon. Dusty was an easygoing pony, and he accepted Whitestar as the boss, even though the colt was much younger. The two had become fast friends, grazing together and nudging each other affectionately. They hated to be parted at the end of the day, but Jason didn't dare leave his pony at the cabin. Dusty would definitely have been missed at the Colby ranch.

Tracy was content just being with Whitestar, grooming and exercising him and knowing the colt had learned to love and trust her. Their hours in the meadow became a game as they trotted in circles and figure eights. Every so often Whitestar would nudge her with his head like a playful puppy, and Tracy would feel a burst of happiness.

But Jason wasn't satisfied with simply caring for the colt. He wanted to start training him, and he talked Tracy into letting him try getting Whitestar used to a bridle. Jason did know what he was doing, and Tracy watched with fascination as he picked up an old bridle he'd brought from his ranch and approached the colt.

First Jason dropped the reins over the colt's neck. He used them to hold the colt as he took off Whitestar's halter. Then he eased the bridle over Whitestar's muzzle until the bit was touching the colt's lips.

Whitestar had gotten so used to Jason that he didn't shy away from Jason's assured touch. The colt had also gotten used to wearing the halter, so he didn't object to the leather bands of the bridle as Jason drew it on.

The bit was something else again. Whitestar had no intention of opening his mouth to accept it. It didn't taste or smell like food. But Jason's experience with horses came to his aid. Before the colt realized what was happening, Jason had reached under the colt's lower jaw. He slipped his fingers into the space all horses have between their front and back teeth. In reaction Whitestar opened his mouth. Jason gently pushed in the bit so that it rested in that gap. Then he drew the headpiece of the bridle up over the horse's ears. As Whitestar chomped on this new metal object in his mouth, Jason fastened the throatstrap. Whitestar continued playing with the bit, but he made no other objections. Jason brought the reins back over the colt's head and led him toward the others. He was grinning over his success.

"We can't do much more until someone rides him," he said. "But at least he'll be getting used to the bridle."

"You made it look so easy," Tracy exclaimed.

"That was the easiest part. The hard part will be getting him used to a saddle. Then we can teach him neck-reining. I can't wait!"

Deep in her heart Tracy wanted to keep training him, too, but she knew the dangers. She shouldn't start acting as if they were going to keep Whitestar. Someday they were going to have to set him free, even if she kept pushing that date farther and farther into the future.

They did continue using the bridle, however. Tracy learned how to put it on Whitestar by herself with Jason instructing her. The first few times she had trouble getting Whitestar to take the bit, but soon she was doing the task with assurance. Tracy used the reins now to lead the colt through his exercises. She imitated the twists and turns a cow pony would make, but, of course, it wasn't the same as actually riding the colt.

"I've got an idea!" Jason said one afternoon as they were sitting in the meadow watching Whitestar and Dusty graze. "Come over to my place tomorrow and see how a trained cow pony works. My dad wouldn't mind. I could even let you try riding. We've got a real quiet old mare who'd be great for someone who's never ridden before."

Tracy had only been to the Colby ranch once before, when she'd gone over with Colin. He and Jason had spent the whole afternoon painting lead figures of knights and monsters, and she'd hardly gotten to see the horses at all. "Do you mean it—I could try riding?"

"Sure. Colin could, too."

Colin was nodding his head eagerly.

"Okay, let's!" Tracy said. "We could finish

up our chores before lunch, check on Whitestar, and then come over."

Tracy's stomach was jumping in excitement as she and Colin hurried down from the cabin early the next afternoon. They had planned on riding their bikes over to Jason's since they didn't have a horse to carry them back and forth over the three miles to the Colby ranch. But when they told Emily where they were going, she offered to give them a ride.

"I was going into town anyway to get my hair cut. Why don't I pick you up on my way back? That'll give me a chance to visit Jason's mom."

Jason was waiting impatiently by the corral when Emily dropped Tracy and Colin off. He waved and grinned, and the two of them hurried over. Tracy's eyes glowed as she got a good look at the horses. There were about a dozen in the grassy enclosure.

"This is about half of them," Jason explained. "We keep them in here when they're not being used. But come on. We're lucky. They're cutting some cattle out in one of the pastures. You can watch the guys work."

Tracy and Colin hurried after Jason, who ran off toward a stand of trees. On the other side of the trees was a large, fenced pasture, and out toward the middle two mounted cowhands were busy at work amid a herd of red-and-white Herefords. Two others were on the ground near a smaller fenced pen with a swinging gate.

"Now watch," Jason instructed. "The horse and rider work like a team. They've got to cut out certain cattle and drive them into the pen without spooking the whole herd."

One of the riders went into action. Tracy had no idea which cow he was singling out, but his horse obviously did. The horse dove in among the herd, then suddenly turned, cutting one cow away. The cow tried to get back to the herd, but the horse spun with him, blocking his path and driving him farther out. Every move the cow made, the horse echoed. The cow had no choice but to move toward the pen, where the two hands were waiting to swing open the gate. A few dozen yards from the gate, the cow made one last attempt to move off to the right. The horse spun and circled that way, cutting him off. In two more quick maneuvers the horse had the protesting cow through the gate, and the hands swung it shut.

Of course, Tracy knew that the horse wasn't doing all the work. The rider was giving him commands.

Jason must have been reading her mind. "Do you know," he said, "that most of the experienced ponies will cut like that without even having a rider in the saddle?"

"Pretty amazing," she agreed.

They stayed to watch a few more cows being cut, then Jason urged them on. "If you want to try riding, then we better get going. I've already got Rosey out of the corral. We just have to saddle her."

"Rosey's the old mare?" Tracy asked.

"Yeah. You'll like her. She used to be one of Dad's best ponies, but he decided to retire her a couple of years ago. My mother rides her sometimes so she doesn't get too fat and lazy."

When they'd reached the barn near the corral, Jason went inside and returned with the mare. She was a pretty dapple-gray and not much bigger than a pony. She studied Tracy from under long, silky eyelashes.

"Hi, Rosey," Tracy said. She patted the mare's neck. The mare stood placid and peaceful, but butterflies were fluttering in Tracy's stomach.

"Here, hold her while I get the saddle," Jason said.

Tracy didn't know why she was so nervous. She'd wanted to learn to ride for as long as she could remember. Maybe that was why doing well seemed especially important.

"She looks real gentle," Colin said as though to reassure himself.

Jason returned and quickly saddled the mare. He then took the reins from Tracy. "I'll lead her around first. Then you can try her on your own. Go ahead, mount up."

Tracy had seen enough riders and read enough books to know that she should mount on the horse's left side. She put her foot in the stirrup and reached for the saddle horn.

"You never grab the horn to mount," Jason said. "Put your right hand on the seat of the saddle and your left hand on top of her neck. Then hop up and swing your leg over."

Tracy did as she was told and soon was sitting firmly in the saddle. She put her right foot in the other stirrup and tried to relax. Her instinct was to grab for the horn and hold on, but she knew better than that.

"Here we go." Jason led the mare off at a walk, up and down the drive and around the packed dirt area in front of the barn. Tracy loved every minute of it and quickly adjusted to the rocking motion of the horse beneath her. "Okay, now we're going to trot," Jason said. "You've got to sit deep in the saddle. It's going to be pretty bouncy."

Jason wasn't kidding. Tracy had a small shock when she felt the rougher pace. She felt like a sack of grain being bounced up and down and was ready to reach for the horn again to keep from falling off. She caught herself in time and concentrated instead on balancing with her body and legs. She started to get the hang of it, but she was still relieved when Jason slowed to a walk.

He brought the reins over Rosey's head and handed them to Tracy. "Try her yourself. You hold the reins in your left hand in front of the horn. Don't pull on them, but don't leave them too slack, either. When you want her to go right, bring the reins over her neck to the right. To go left, bring them left. To stop, pull back a little, then let go. To get her to start walking, squeeze her a little with your legs, then relax. If you want to trot, you tighten your legs while she's walking and don't let up until she breaks into a jog. You can tap her flanks with your heels, too, but it's better if you just use the leg pressure."

Tracy nodded, trying to remember everything Jason had said. It shouldn't be too hard—at a walk, anyway. Jason stepped back. Tracy squeezed with her legs and then released the pressure. The mare started forward at a walk up the drive. Tracy felt a brief jolt of panic when she realized it was just Rosey and her. If Rosey should decide to do something unexpected, Tracy would have to handle the situation all by herself.

Rosey was too complacent and well-trained to surprise her rider, though. She proceeded at a steady walking pace up the drive. Tracy was relaxing more and more. She kept her shoulders and back straight, but let herself go with the rhythm of the horse.

At the same place in the drive where Jason had turned, Tracy brought the reins over the mare's neck to the right. Around they went . . . and around . . . in a nice tight circle. Tracy suddenly realized she'd forgotten to release the pressure of the reins after the turn!

When they were again facing the barn, Tracy brought the reins back to the center of the mare's neck, and grinned at her success when they moved forward in a straight line.

She rode six circuits around the drive and had screwed up her courage to try the next circuit at a trot. She was just about to head up the drive again, when Emily drove in through the gates. She smiled broadly when she saw Tracy on horseback, and after she'd parked the car, she hurried over.

"Don't you look great! You didn't tell me you were learning to ride."

"Today's the first lesson."

"You're doing real well. Is Colin going to try, too?"

"I sure am," Colin shouted, "if Tracy *ever* gets off."

Emily laughed. "You've got another half hour. I'll go talk to Sally, but then I've got to head back to start dinner."

Tracy hated to stop. She was just getting the feel of what it was like to ride, and was already dreaming of what it would be like to be riding Whitestar instead of the mare. But it wouldn't be fair to Colin if she continued. She'd already been riding over a half an hour. Reluctantly she brought the mare over to the boys and dismounted.

Jason went through the same procedure with Colin, and Tracy leaned back against the corral fence to watch. She carried on with her daydream, imagining Whitestar in bridle and saddle with her aboard. Of course, it wouldn't be so easy with Whitestar. He wouldn't be docile and accepting like Rosey. He'd very likely display some playful and mischievous antics. Only an experienced rider could handle him. Tracy would need many more lessons and hours in the saddle before she could even think about getting up on Whitestar's back.

If she owned Whitestar, it would be different. Jason could ride well enough to break the colt, and if Tracy kept practicing on Rosey . . .

Tracy shook her head. What good did it do to let her imagination run wild? There wasn't a chance that any of her dreams would come true. Even if Whitestar hadn't been a mustang, her father wouldn't have let her keep the horse—he wouldn't allow any horses at the ranch. She wondered what he'd say about their riding at Jason's. Would he be mad about that, too?

On the way home she asked Emily.

"Well, it's true he doesn't like horses much. He might be a little worried that you'll get hurt . . . though I don't see that happening with that gentle old mare. Are you going to keep riding?"

"I don't know. If Jason doesn't mind. I really like it!" At that moment Tracy wished more than anything that she could tell Emily about Whitestar, but she didn't dare.

Emily never mentioned Tracy and Colin's riding lesson to their father at dinner that night. Maybe she'd decided not to tell him at all. Their father had plenty of ranch business to talk about anyway.

Tracy listened with half an ear, waiting in dread for her father to mention ranch business that wasn't so pleasant—the coyotes, or the mustangs. He didn't say a word about them, though, and he left the house right after dinner to look over some of the sheep. As soon as Tracy and Colin had finished up the dishes, they headed up the mountain to the cabin.

"You'd like to try some more riding lessons, wouldn't you?" Tracy asked her brother as they walked up through the woods.

"I sure would. It was really neat! How 'bout you?"

"I'm going to ask Jason tomorrow. I don't

think Emily will tell Dad. Oh, Colin, wouldn't it be fun?"

"But Jason's going to be gone all next week," Colin said. "Remember? We can't ask him."

Tracy's shoulders sagged in disappointment. "I forgot. He's going to visit his grandmother in Cheyenne. Darn! Well, we'll ask him when he gets back." Tracy's expression immediately brightened. "I'm sure he'll say it's okay." The taste of riding that day had only sparked her appetite to learn more—and it had made her want to keep Whitestar all the more, too.

Eight

Tracy never imagined she'd ever miss Jason, but in the next few days she did. She occupied her time with Whitestar. After seeing the horses at Jason's ranch, she realized just how beautiful the colt was. If he were trained, he'd stand out like a shining star.

On those hot afternoons, she lay on her stomach in the long grass watching Colin take his turn exercising the colt. She pictured herself on the colt's back, in a silver decorated saddle. She imagined them parading around the show ring at the annual rodeo. The viewers in the stands would applaud this beautiful horse and his rider. She'd have a black outfit, with silver spangles on the pockets and fringe on the sleeves. And a black hat with a silver band. Her boots would shine as brightly as Whitestar's coat. What a wonderful team they'd make, racing around barrels, cutting corners, twirling and spinning, and coming over the finish line in the best time.

Her daydreams made Tracy impatient. She couldn't wait for Jason to return. She decided to start trying to break the colt on her own by getting him used to the feel of a blanket on his back. She shook out the blanket that Shag had been using and folded it to the approximate size of a saddle blanket. While the colt grazed behind the cabin she gently placed the folded blanket on his back. He was busy eating and didn't seem to notice for a minute.

Then his back muscles twitched—and twitched again more violently. He finally shook himself all over, and the blanket fell to the ground. Tracy picked it up. She wasn't ready to admit defeat.

She untied the colt and started him walking up the trail to the meadow. She had the folded blanket ready in one hand, and when they were halfway up the trail, she quickly slid it onto the colt's back. His muscles rippled immediately, but she urged him forward.

"Look, Whitestar, we're almost to the meadow!" Tracy cried, trying to distract him.

The trick worked. He forgot about the object on his back as he saw the tall grass of the meadow. He walked contentedly beside her with his ears pricked forward in anticipation. They circled the meadow together at a walk, following their well-worn path. Then she trotted him. The blanket stayed in place, even when Whitestar grew more playful. He knew their routine and was eager as Tracy led him around imaginary barrels, through loops and turns. He loved every minute of it—lifting his hooves high and shaking his head in pleasure.

When Whitestar seemed satisfied with his exercise, Tracy slowed him to a walk. He nudged her gently with his velvet nose as if to say thank you. She rubbed her hand behind his ears. "You're wonderful, Whitestar. Do you know that?" Tracy let him graze on the thick meadow grass as a reward. The folded blanket was still on his back, and Tracy felt she'd taken a big step that day.

Of course, there was a lot more to do if she were ever going to ride him. She had to train herself to ride first. But how she loved him! And how he was beginning to love her!

The day finally came when Jason was due home. Tracy and Colin spent that morning cleaning out one of the sheep pens near the barn. Tracy looked up from loading the wheelbarrow to see Jenks heading up the mountain road in the Jeep.

She nudged Colin. "Look! There goes Jenks. I'll bet he's putting out more traps!"

Colin frowned as he watched the cloud of dust churned up by the Jeep's tires. "Maybe not. Dad moved some of the sheep to the high meadows. Jenks might just be going to check them. It's faster in the Jeep."

"It's not just the traps," Tracy said nervously. "Haven't you seen the funny looks he's been giving us? He knows we're up to something. What if he goes checking and finds Whitestar?"

"He won't go way over there. The high meadows aren't anywhere near the cabin."

Tracy knew Colin was right, but she hurried through her chores so she could get up to see the colt. Whitestar was fine when she arrived that afternoon, and there was no sign of anyone having been near the cabin.

She'd already mucked out the cabin by the time Colin, Jason, and Dusty came up the path. Whitestar greeted Dusty with a welcoming whinny. He'd missed the other horse.

Jason was full of stories of his trip. After he tied Dusty beside the colt, he jabbered on about Cheyenne and the rodeo his grandmother had taken him to see.

"I liked the steer roping the best," he said with excitement. "You would have liked the races, Tracy. Boy, could those quarter horses go!"

"What about the bronc riding?" Colin asked.

"I don't know—I think it's kind of mean. They tie a strap under the horse's belly to make him buck like that."

"It doesn't really hurt them, does it?" Colin worried.

"It's still not very nice."

Tracy finally managed to get in a word. "Wait till you see what I did while you were gone," she said to Jason. "I got Whitestar used to having a blanket on his back."

"Oh, yeah? Show me."

Tracy ran and got the blanket. She wanted to impress Jason and hoped that Whitestar would behave as well as he had during the last few days. She didn't have to worry. Whitestar hardly reacted at all when she laid the blanket on his back. He walked along happily as they all went up to the meadow. Tracy then took Whitestar through his paces.

"Not bad," Jason complimented her when they were finished. "What we've got to do now is try him with a saddle."

Tracy's interest perked. "You mean it? How are we going to get one?" she asked.

"We could use Dusty's."

Why hadn't Tracy thought of that? "Today?"

"If you want. We could put it on his back like you did with the blanket until he gets used to the weight. I wouldn't try to cinch it right away."

"Let's do it!" Tracy was eager to try, though she knew that the colt would find the saddle much harder to get used to. She had a feeling he would buck it off.

She held Whitestar as Jason removed the saddle from Dusty. He tied up the cinch so it wouldn't hang down under Whitestar's belly and brought the stirrups up over the seat of the saddle. Then he walked over with the saddle in his arms and let the colt see it and sniff it.

"Okay," he instructed Tracy, "you just hold him. I'll put it on his back."

Tracy spoke quietly to Whitestar and rubbed his nose as Jason approached his side and lifted the saddle. Very slowly, Jason lowered it onto the middle of the colt's back. When the saddle was in place, Jason quickly stepped back.

Whitestar stood perfectly still for about ten seconds. Only his ears flicked around. Then he snorted, and with a twisting half-buck tried to dislodge this strange and unexpected weight on his back. There was nothing to hold the saddle in place, and it immediately slid off. Whitestar sidestepped away from it. He stared at the heap on the ground from the corner of his eye and shook his head vigorously.

Tracy had to laugh. "You didn't like that one bit, did you, boy? But it's not so bad. Dusty wears one. He doesn't mind."

Of course, the colt didn't understand her words, but he knew the soothing tone of her voice. He stopped fidgeting. But when Jason picked up the saddle again and started in his direction, he immediately sidestepped away, moving in a circle around Tracy.

"Let me try," she said. "He knows me better."

Jason shrugged. He obviously didn't think Tracy could do any better. He came and took the lead rope, and Tracy picked up the saddle.

"This isn't going to hurt, Whitestar," she said as she approached. "Easy . . . easy. That's a boy. Just hold still." The saddle was heavy, but Tracy slowly hoisted it up over the colt's back, then gently lowered it in place. She immediately reached out to rub her hand over the colt's neck. "See, it's not so bad. It's just some old leather. You don't have to buck it off." The colt stood in place, and Tracy continued rubbing his neck and talking to him. His ears flicked around as he listened to her. She waited for the explosion and was ready to jump out of the way. But her soft words and touch seemed to work miracles. Whitestar allowed the saddle to remain in place.

A full minute passed before Tracy expelled her breath in a sigh of relief. She carefully stepped forward, keeping a hand on the colt's neck and talking to him. When she reached his head, she took the lead rope from Jason. Still talking to the horse, she led him forward a few steps.

Tracy expected the fireworks to start. Whitestar gave a few uneasy snorts. Tracy could sense the tension in his muscles, yet he continued to walk forward beside her with the saddle on his back. She hardly believed her luck as she led him away from the boys and around their familiar circle in the meadow. The colt grew less tense as they walked. Tracy could tell that he still wasn't certain about the added weight on his back, but he didn't try to get rid of the saddle.

She kept her fingers crossed until they'd gone all the way around the meadow. She stopped Whitestar beside the boys, then turned and wrapped her arms around the colt's neck.

"You're wonderful!" she cried. "Good boy. That wasn't so bad, was it?"

"I don't believe it," Jason said when Tracy looked up. "He sure trusts you."

Tracy only smiled. "But that's enough for today."

"Pretty good for one day," Jason responded. "Maybe my dad ought to hire you to break all his colts."

"It's only because Whitestar knows me." Tracy laughed at the suggestion.

"He knows us, too," Jason persisted. "He must think you're pretty special."

Tracy looked at him, tongue-tied, as an unfamiliar blush warmed her cheeks.

"Tracy spends more time with him," Colin reminded Jason. "It's like he's gotten to be her horse."

"I suppose," Jason agreed. "Too bad you don't know how to ride, Tracy."

"I was going to ask you," Tracy said, quickly

recovering from her embarrassment. "Do you think Colin and I could keep coming over to your place and learn to ride on Rosey? I wouldn't dare try to ride Whitestar unless I knew a lot more."

Jason didn't hesitate with his answer. His eyes lit up as he answered enthusiastically. "Sure! I'd like to teach you, and Rosey needs the exercise. We can keep training Whitestar, too. By the end of the summer, maybe you'll be good enough to ride him yourself!"

Of course, Tracy didn't want to think about the end of summer, or of how quickly the days were going by. She'd already kept Whitestar longer than she'd intended. What they needed was a miracle. But the idea of actually riding Whitestar brought a wide smile to her face.

Tracy held the colt, and Jason removed the saddle. The colt rippled his back muscles, glad to have the weight gone. He seemed to be telling Tracy that he'd only put up with it because of her.

"Do you want to come riding tomorrow?" Jason asked. He resaddled Dusty, who'd been patiently cropping the grass.

"Sure," Tracy and Colin said in one breath.

"Come over after lunch then. I'll have Rosey ready."

Tracy gave Jason an impulsive hug. "You're great! Thanks a lot, Jason."

Jason's cheeks flushed crimson at the compliment. He looked down at his boots to hide his embarrassment. "It's okay."

Nine

Tracy and Colin's riding lesson the next day went fine. By the end of her hour, Tracy had Rosey going at a nice even trot and was improving her own seat in the saddle. Colin did almost as well, but Tracy had more of an incentive to learn to ride as quickly as possible.

In the following days they alternated their time between Jason's and the cabin, where they continued Whitestar's lessons. The colt had progressed to the point that he now allowed the cinch of the saddle to be loosely fastened. The next step would be a rider, but Tracy wanted to give him more time. Her goal was to be his first rider, and she needed a lot more practice on Rosey first.

"How's the riding going?" Emily asked that afternoon when they rode their bikes back from Jason's after their lesson.

"Great." Tracy parked her bike and grinned. "We tried a canter today. It's a lot more comfortable than a trot because you don't bounce around so much! We're going to practice it some more next lesson."

"It's nice of Jason to teach you. I'm glad you're having such a good time, but remember on Friday you've both got dentist appointments in town. Don't make any plans for that afternoon."

They both wrinkled their noses. "Yuk," Colin said.

"It's only for a cleaning and a fluoride treatment," Emily said. "That's painless."

The visit to the dentist might be painless, but to Tracy it meant that they'd miss a valuable afternoon with Whitestar. She'd have to get her chores done in record time if she wanted to spend any time with the colt beforehand.

Tracy was growing expert at bridling and saddling Whitestar. Jason had showed her how to place the saddle blanket and tie the cinch. Leading Whitestar by the reins, she now took him around the meadow and through loops and turns with the saddle on his back. Each day her dream of riding him seemed closer to becoming true. She'd made up her mind that after her next lesson with Rosey on Thursday, she was going to try to sit in the saddle on Whitestar's back. She felt the colt trusted her. He just might let her sit on his back without bucking her off. She wouldn't try to ride him—only let him get used to her weight. She knew he was still too young to ride regularly. She was filled with anticipation, and each night she fell asleep with that dream in mind.

By Friday, Tracy had forgotten about their dentist appointments. She didn't remember until Emily reminded her at lunchtime that they would have to leave for town at one. She only had time for a quick run up to the cabin to check on the colt.

Jenks was coming out of the barn as Tracy ran off, but she was in too much of a hurry to give it a thought. There wasn't time to exercise the colt, but she groomed him and gave him fresh water, then hurtled back down to the ranch. Emily and Colin were already heading for the car when Tracy joined them.

"Hoping to miss your dentist appointment?" Emily teased.

"Well, it's not exactly fun."

"We'll stop for an ice cream in town afterward. Is that a good enough bribe?" Emily asked, laughing.

They didn't get back from town until close to five. As soon as they turned in the ranch drive, Tracy knew something had happened. The hands were all gathered near the barn and were talking excitedly among themselves.

"I wonder what's up?" Emily said in a worried voice. She parked the car quickly, and the three of them jumped out and hurried toward the huddled men.

"Randy, what's wrong?" Emily called to the ranch hand standing nearest them.

In answer he lifted his hand and pointed beyond the barn to one of the sheep pens that had been empty that morning. Tracy couldn't see over the heads of the ranch hands. She pushed through the crowd with Emily and Colin behind her. She felt her stomach tightening in dread. Instinctively she knew that she wasn't going to like what she saw.

Finally she reached the side of the pen. Her worst fears were confirmed. Inside was a very frightened, rearing horse—Whitestar!

"No!" Tracy screamed. She climbed up the lower rail of the pen in time to see Jenks fastening the gate at the other side. "Whitestar! Whitestar!" she cried. With all the commotion, her voice didn't carry. The colt didn't hear her. He reared up again. His eyes were wild with panic. Tracy felt her own eyes fill with frightened and angry tears.

Colin scrambled up beside her. His face was pale, and his voice was choked. "They found him . . . oh, Tracy!"

The colt had stopped rearing and stood sweating and trembling in the middle of the pen. He was terrified by all the staring faces and loud voices.

"Not a bad-looking stallion for a mustang," one of the hands muttered.

"Wouldn't want to be in those kids' shoes, though," another answered. "They're in for it when Mr. Jordan finds out."

Tracy barely heard their voices. Her attention was focused on Whitestar. A rope still dangled from around his neck. Another rope was fastened to his halter. Both ropes swung wildly as he suddenly spun in his tracks and raced toward the back of the pen, away from the men. He was desperately searching for a way out. But there was none, and he ran up and down along the rear fence, snorting and neighing for help.

Tracy's heart wrenched at the sight of the terrified colt. She had to help him! He needed her. He'd learned to trust her. She couldn't let this happen to him!

She cried out to him again, and this time her voice rose above the noises around her. The colt suddenly stopped his mad dash along the rear fence. His ears pricked, and he turned his head in her direction.

The men around her grew silent when they saw the change in the colt.

"Whitestar!" Tracy shouted again. "I'm here, boy!"

The colt saw her. He gave a joyous whinny and started forward. Then he stopped in his tracks as he saw the other men crowded behind Tracy. They were his enemies. He wouldn't go to Tracy while they were there. He trembled in nervousness and blew anxious breaths through his nose.

Tracy knew she had to go to him. In two quick moves, she scaled the top of the fence and jumped inside the pen. Her voice was a soothing murmur as she slowly walked toward the colt.

"Easy . . . easy, Whitestar. It's me, your friend. I won't let anything happen to you . . . I promise."

The colt's ears remained forward, tuned in to the sound of her voice. It was a voice he knew and trusted—a voice that meant kindness and love. He was still frightened. He wouldn't come any closer, but he didn't retreat, either. He stood in place until Tracy was a few feet away. Then he gently nickered.

"Oh, Whitestar!" Tracy crossed the last few feet and threw her arms around the colt's neck. He turned his head and nudged her shoulder in relief and happiness. For several minutes they stood together. Neither of them were aware of anything or anyone else. The group around the pen had grown completely silent. Everyone stared at the girl and mustang in amazement.

Tracy carefully slid the rope off Whitestar's neck. She was about to unfasten his halter rope, too, when a loud voice broke the silence. Whitestar reacted as if he'd been slapped. His head jerked up, and his muscles tensed. Tracy felt her happiness crumbling around her.

"Get out of that pen right now!" her father ordered. She turned and saw him standing at the edge of the fence beside Colin. His face was like a thundercloud. She'd never seen him so angry, but there was something else in his expression, too. He seemed frightened.

When Tracy didn't move or respond, he called out again. "Did you hear me? Get away from that horse! He's a wild animal. Get out of here—*now!*"

Tracy finally managed to choke out some words. "He won't hurt me. He needs me."

"Jenks, go in there and get her," Tracy's father ordered.

Tracy's face went white. She couldn't let Jenks come into the pen and further frighten Whitestar. She didn't have any choice but to do what her father said. With a soothing hand, she tried to quiet the colt. "Don't be afraid, boy," she pleaded. "I'll be back. I won't let them hurt you."

Reluctantly she left Whitestar's side and started toward the fence. He whinnied to her anxiously, not wanting her to go. She looked back over her shoulder, and tears rose to blur her vision. The colt seemed to be begging her with his eyes not to leave him. She sniffed back a sob and continued on to the fence. Her father practically lifted her over. He'd no sooner put her on her feet on the other side than his voice rose in anger.

"You little sneaks—you and your brother! Hiding that miserable mustang up in the woods and never saying a word to anyone! You know how I feel about these mustangs. Yet you deliberately disobeyed me! It's a good thing Jenks had enough sense to know you two were up to something. I ought to tan both your bottoms!"

The crowd around them had begun backing away. The men didn't want to be a part of the family argument.

"Dad, please—" Tracy begged. "He was hurt. We had to save him!"

"Save him for what? So he could go out and eat up all my pastureland, cause trouble? He's nothing but a worthless nag! But you and your brother sneaking behind my back is worse. I suppose Jason Colby was in on it, too, since he's been around the ranch so much. I'll be having a word with his father!"

"Dad, don't be so mad," Colin cried. "We couldn't let him die. He was caught in some fence wire. It was wrapped around his leg and he couldn't get loose. We had to take care of him until his leg healed. We were going to set him free—"

"I'm not interested in your excuses. You both knew what you should have done—and that was to come straight down here when you found him and tell me about it. One of the hands would have taken care of it."

"By sending him off to be butchered?" Tracy said coldly. "Like all the other mustangs you've captured?"

"That's all they're worth!" her father shot back.

"They're worth more than that. Whitestar especially! Look how beautiful he is. We love him—and we've started to train him. He trusts us."

"It took three hands to get that mean piece of horseflesh off the mountain! Don't talk to me about training him. You can't train a mustang. They'll always be wild and mean."

"The men frightened him. He knew they were going to hurt him. He doesn't act that way with us. Didn't you just see?"

"That's enough out of you, young lady. You disobeyed me and lied to me. The two of you are grounded. I'll take care of that mustang. Get in the house and stay in your rooms!"

"Dad, please . . ." Tracy's throat felt hoarse.

"Do as I say. I'll be in to see both of you later."

Tracy was beside herself. Whitestar's dilemma was all her fault! If she hadn't been so selfish and had let him go as soon as he had healed, he wouldn't be standing in the pen, doomed to a horrible fate.

She felt an arm go around her shoulder and heard Emily speak. "Marty, please. Don't you think you're being a little too hard on them? Maybe they were wrong to hide the horse, but they did it out of kindness."

"You know how I feel about mustangs, Emily."

"I know, but this is different. They care about this animal. They've given a lot of themselves to save it. It's not just another wild horse. Can't you reconsider—"

"The horse goes, and that's final!" Still angry, their father spun on his heel and walked away.

Emily put an arm around each of the crying children. "Come on, kids. I'll try to talk to your father when he calms down. He does have a right to be angry, you know."

"But we *love* Whitestar! What else could we do?"

"I know. Maybe there's still some hope." Emily tried to reassure them, but she didn't sound very hopeful herself.

She walked with them to Tracy's bedroom. "I know it's hard, but try to understand your father. He loves you both very much, and it hurts him to find out you've been lying. It hurts him, too, to have one of the hands tell him that his kids have been sneaking behind his back."

"I just don't understand, Emily," Tracy cried.

"Why does Dad hate mustangs so much? He doesn't hate other animals. He traps the coyotes, but that's only because he's afraid for the sheep—not because he hates them."

Emily sighed, then sat down on the edge of the bed. She motioned to Tracy and Colin to sit down, too. "Your father won't talk about it, but I guess it's time somebody told you what happened. He didn't always hate mustangs. In fact, he and his father used to train the mustangs they rounded up, and they treated them very well. Your father helped break the horses to saddle and teach them how to cut and herd. The horses that weren't needed on the ranch were sold off to other ranchers, who used them as cow ponies.

"I used to come over and ride with your father and grandfather sometimes. Your father was a wonderful rider and competed in the local rodeos. Then one day when he was about fourteen, his father was breaking a mustang stallion that had been brought down to the ranch with several mares a few days before. The stallion was a real beauty, but he was incredibly spirited and strong-minded. Your grandfather always used gentleness to tame a horse—just like you've done with that colt outside. The horses always responded."

Her voice grew sad. "I wasn't there the day the accident happened, but your father was watching from the side of the corral. His father was inside with the stallion. He'd spent the last couple of days teaching the stallion to trust him. He'd gotten as far as getting a halter on the horse. He was talking to the horse, who'd been behaving very well, when suddenly the stallion turned on him. He reared up and caught your grandfather unaware. Your grandfather fell, and the stallion pounded him with his hooves. Your father jumped into the corral and tried to help, but it was too late. By the time he'd frightened the stallion off, the stallion had crushed your grandfather's spine and broken his neck. He died in your father's arms."

Emily paused and sighed sadly. "Your father was never the same after that. When they'd gotten your grandfather out of the corral, your father took a gun and shot the stallion. He sold off every horse on the ranch. He wouldn't talk about the accident to anyone, but since that day, he's hated mustangs. It might be hard for you to understand, but I know how badly he was hurt." She turned to Tracy and Colin. "That's why he's never had horses on the ranch. And that's why he's so determined to get rid of that mustang stallion of yours. I know he's afraid that the same thing could happen again."

Tracy shook her head and swallowed. "If someone had told us, Emily . . ."

"I know. I've wanted to every time you

pleaded for the mustangs, but your father gets so upset whenever someone mentions that accident. It still hurts for him to talk or think about it."

Tracy was beginning to understand her father, but why did Whitestar have to suffer? He hadn't done anything. He wouldn't turn on them. He shouldn't be punished because of what had happened a long time ago. Couldn't her father see that not all horses were dangerous?

"We can't let Whitestar be sent away, Emily. It's not his fault!"

"I know, and I'm going to try very hard to get your father to see it that way." She gave them both a kiss. "I'll talk to your dad tonight and see if I can't get him to change his mind."

"I don't think he will," Colin said through his tears when Emily had left the room. "If I were Dad, I'd probably hate mustangs, too."

"But Whitestar's different, Colin. I can't let Dad send him away. I just can't!"

Ten

Tracy and Colin were allowed out of their bedrooms long enough to eat dinner in the kitchen.

Their father came straight in from his office in the barn. "I hope you kids have had time to do some thinking," he said gruffly as he sat down.

Tracy knew it would be wasted breath to argue for Whitestar's safety. Emily hadn't had a chance to talk to their father yet. She and Colin only dropped their eyes.

"That mustang will be out of here in two days," their father continued. "The trucker can't get here before then. I want you two to stay away from that pen. And that's an order. Don't let me see or hear about you going near that horse!"

That was too much for Tracy. She didn't care what her father thought right then. She pushed her plate away. "Excuse me," she muttered, and rushed off to her bedroom in tears.

She heard her father call after her, telling

her to come back to the table, but she kept going.

"Marty, let her go," Emily said.

That was all Tracy heard of their conversation. She closed her door behind her, collapsed on the bed, and sobbed her heart out. Whitestar had been given a death sentence—and it would be carried out in two days. And it was all her fault. She'd never felt so awful in all her life. She couldn't let the colt die! But what *could* she do? She wasn't even allowed near his pen! She'd think of something—she *had* to. But what?

Colin didn't come into her bedroom. He'd probably been told to stay in his own room. Tracy spent the next two miserable hours all by herself. Her eyes were red and swollen from all her tears. She was tempted to sneak out the window, but she knew that tonight someone would be watching and would catch her. Then her punishment would be even worse—if anything could be worse than knowing Whitestar was going to die.

Tracy was lying on her bed staring at the ceiling when Emily came into the room. Tracy looked up anxiously.

Emily sat down beside Tracy and sadly shook her head. "I tried, Tracy. I'm sorry, but your father's fear and hatred of mustangs goes so deep. He can't forget that it was a mustang stallion who killed his father—and that he saw it

112

happen. He's afraid it could happen to you kids."

"Oh, Emily . . ." Tracy fell into the older woman's arms. Fresh tears sprang up in her already stinging eyes. They rolled unheeded down her cheeks as the housekeeper patted her back.

"Sweetheart, I know how badly you feel. I feel horrible myself. I can see how much that colt means to you. He isn't like the stallion who killed your grandfather." She sighed. "We still have a day. I'll keep trying."

"They're just going to leave Whitestar locked up out there with no one to take care of him or feed him?"

"Your father's not cruel. He'll see that the colt's fed and watered."

Tracy felt as though she were facing her own death sentence. She hurt so badly that she couldn't sleep. All she could do was think of Whitestar and all the wonderful times they'd had together. She went to the kitchen window and stared across to the pen. Whitestar stood in the center. He looked as dejected and lost as she felt. She longed to go out to him, but her father was in the barn. She couldn't even sneak out.

Jason came by late in the morning. He was as miserable as Tracy and Colin. They went to Colin's bedroom to talk.

"Your dad called mine yesterday. My dad was pretty mad."

"Because you were using up his supplies?" Tracy exclaimed.

"Naw—because I helped you guys sneak behind your father's back. He said I should have stayed out of it. It wasn't my business. Or else I should have brought the colt over to our place at the start."

Tracy jumped at his words. Her expression suddenly brightened. "He would have taken Whitestar? Would he take him now? If he called my dad—"

"I already asked him." Jason sighed unhappily. "He told your dad he'd take the colt. Your dad said no—that he wasn't interested in saving any mustang stallions."

"But Whitestar's going to die!"

"My dad feels bad too, but he said he can't interfere. He doesn't want any hard feelings between him and your dad. We're neighbors and all."

Tracy was desperate. "We could sneak Whitestar over at night—make it look like Whitestar escaped."

"Your dad would find out he was at our place . . . and then there'd be trouble."

Tracy tried to swallow back her renewed disappointment. She felt close to tears again. "There's got to be something we can do!"

114

"What?" Colin asked. "We're not allowed by the pen, and someone's probably watching it anyway."

They all shook their heads dejectedly. Then there was a knock on the door, and Emily came in.

"I shouldn't be doing this," she said, "but I can't stand to see you kids so unhappy. No one's out near the pen. I just checked. Go out and see the colt for a few minutes. He looks pretty lonesome and unhappy himself."

Tracy was off the bed in a flash. She hugged Emily. "Oh, thanks—thanks!"

"If your father or one of the hands comes back, I'll tell them I told you it was okay."

The three of them raced out of the bedroom, down the hall, and out into the yard. Tracy knew, even as she rushed to Whitestar, that seeing the colt might only make things worse for her in the end. But she had to see him. She couldn't stand the thought of him suffering by himself, confused and frightened by his new surroundings.

Whitestar's distress was obvious. From the distance she could see him pacing along the boundaries of the pen, still searching for a way out. She called to him. He immediately spun around and gave a joyous whinny.

In a few strides, Tracy was at the fence. The colt trotted toward her and pushed his head over the top fence board, nudging her in delight.

"Oh, Whitestar," she cried. "Yes, I'm glad to see you, too. Poor baby." Tracy quickly climbed the fence and jumped down beside the colt, flinging her arms around his neck, rubbing his ears and nose. "We didn't want to leave you all alone. You've been frightened . . . and so have I."

The colt nickered his relief to have his friends with him again. Colin and Jason climbed into the pen after Tracy and took turns petting the colt.

Jason pulled a sugar cube from his pocket and fed it to the colt. "I always carry some for Dusty," he explained.

As the three of them gave the colt some much-needed attention, Emily came to stand at the fence. She watched them with a sad smile.

Tracy finally looked up and saw her. "See, Emily. He's not mean or wild. He loves us. He'd never hurt us."

Emily nodded. "Yes, I can see that, Tracy. I wish your father could see it, too."

"Watch this, Emily." In her excitement, Tracy momentarily forgot Whitestar's death sentence and that one of the hands could return at any moment. She took Whitestar's halter and started leading him around the pen. First she walked him, then trotted him, then took him through a series of figure eights. The colt picked up his feet, showing off his beautiful lines and movements, glad to be at play with his friend once again. Tracy's face was glowing. "He can do it with a bridle and saddle, too," she called. "Next we were going to try riding him."

Emily nodded. There were tears in her eyes. "You've done a wonderful job."

Tracy released the colt's halter, but he followed her anyway as she came back across the pen. He didn't seem to want to let her out of his sight.

The boys were just as eager and as happy as Tracy to be with Whitestar. For a few brief moments they were able to forget the colt's fate. Tracy let herself pretend that everything was going to be all right, that a miracle would happen. It was so wonderful to see the colt happy again, and to see Emily smiling from the fence in approval.

They were all abruptly brought back to reality when the Jeep pulled into the yard carrying Jenks and Mr. Jordan. Mr. Jordan was out of the Jeep before Jenks brought it to a stop, and came racing toward the pen. Emily turned and tried to stop him. He rushed past her to the fence. Tracy didn't think she'd ever forget the expression on his face.

"Get out of that pen! Now! All of you! I told you not to go near the horse!"

"Marty!" Emily cried. "I told them they

could. The colt won't hurt them. He's gentle. They've made a pet of him."

"Pet! A mustang? Emily, you've lost your mind. He's a killer like all the rest of them. He goes in the morning."

The three kids had hurried to the fence and were climbing over. Tracy knew how upset her father was, but still she had to plead Whitestar's case. "It's true, Dad. Please listen. Emily was watching us. She saw how we've trained Whitestar. He won't hurt us. You can't send him away! Please let me show you what we've done with him!"

Whitestar was already pacing again, knowing something was terribly wrong.

"This isn't just another wild mustang." Emily added her pleas to Tracy's. "He's got potential, and he loves these kids."

Mr. Jordan shook his head stubbornly. His eyes were flashing. "You know how I feel about this. We've said everything there is to be said. The horse goes. Jason, you get on home. You two"—he motioned to Tracy and Colin—"in the house! And don't leave your rooms, or there'll be more trouble than you want to think about. Get!"

Sobbing once more, Tracy turned. She couldn't have gotten any words of argument past her lips if she'd tried. Colin followed her with tears on his cheeks, too. Behind them Emily continued to try to persuade their father, but Tracy couldn't stand to listen any more. She knew her father wasn't going to change his mind.

She paced her bedroom. She was crying so hard that she could barely see. She had to save him! She couldn't let him die! It was up to her. But what was she going to do?

An idea was forming in her mind as she paced. She'd been terrified of trying it before. Now she was desperate and didn't care what punishment she received. She was going to set Whitestar free—and she had to do it that night. It was going to break her heart to say good-bye to the colt, but at least she'd be losing him to the wild, and he would live.

She wouldn't tell a soul about her plans—not even Colin. She didn't want him to be punished, too. It wasn't going to be easy. She'd have to wait until the middle of the night, and she couldn't release Whitestar at the ranch. She'd have to take him high up in the meadow above the cabin. They couldn't make a sound until they were well away from the ranch and bunkhouse. One noise, one whinny might wake the dogs or the hands. She'd need a flashlight and a lead rope. There was a flashlight in her backpack, but did she dare go into the barn for the lead? It was too risky. She'd have to lead the colt with just a hand on his halter.

Tracy knew the route they'd take. They'd

follow the line of sheep pens until they were around the bend in the mountain road, then cut across the woods toward the trail to the cabin. The going would be rough through the woods, but she'd make it. Whitestar's life depended on it!

Her plans were firm in her mind, but now she had the agonizing hours to wait until she could carry them through. The rest of the day seemed to stretch out endlessly in front of her. And what if her father, in his anger, had gotten the trucker to come sooner? No! She wouldn't think of that. The truck would be there in the morning, but by then, Whitestar would be running free.

Eleven

Tracy didn't want to arouse suspicion. She stayed in her room all afternoon, but she fidgeted, and paced, and wished for the hours to go faster. Emily came in before dinner.

"Are you all right, sweetheart?" she asked.

Tracy shrugged. What could she say? She was miserable, but now that she'd made her plans for Whitestar, she had something to relieve her pain.

"Your father's upset about all of this, too," Emily added. "He said he won't be in for dinner tonight. He's going to work late in his office. When he does that it usually means he's got a lot on his mind." Emily paused. "You know that he doesn't mean to hurt you or Colin."

"I know, but—"

"That doesn't make you feel much better, though, does it?"

"No," Tracy said honestly.

"Come on out for dinner. It'll be ready in a few minutes."

"I'm not very hungry."

"You have to eat something."

121

"All right," Tracy said reluctantly.

Dinner turned out to be a silent meal. Neither Tracy nor Colin had anything to say, and Emily understood their moods. Tracy realized that it was worse for Colin. He didn't know about her plan for releasing Whitestar and that there was still a chance of saving the colt. She was very tempted to tell him, but in the end she decided she had to win or fail at the task alone.

After dinner she tried to rest for a few hours. She put on her pajamas in case her father checked on her. She set her alarm for two in the morning and climbed into bed, but she couldn't sleep. She tossed and turned and mentally rehearsed every step of her plan. The hours dragged. The hands of her alarm clock seemed to move so slowly.

By one-thirty, Tracy couldn't stand it any longer. She got up and dressed in the dark in her jeans and a sweater, and pulled on her boots. She slid the flashlight under the belt of her jeans, then pushed open the screen of her bedroom window.

Before climbing out she listened. She didn't hear any noises except the usual night sounds—the constant hum of the peepers and the distant, sleepy baa of a sheep. Carefully she slid out of the window feetfirst and dropped silently to the ground. She checked to make sure there were no lights burning in her father's bedroom, then edged her way along the back of the house and around the corner.

A quarter moon lit the sky. It gave out enough light for Tracy to distinguish shadowy shapes. Her eyes were already adjusted to the darkness, and that meager light was enough. She didn't dare use her flashlight until she and Whitestar were away from the ranch buildings.

Tracy moved toward the front of the house and looked across the yard to the barn and bunkhouse. A single light burned over the bunkhouse door. Everything else was dark and still. Her eyes went to Whitestar's pen, but she couldn't see beyond the wide-board fence.

On tiptoe she edged across the yard toward the pen. The next steps of her plan were so important and could mean success or failure. She had to unlatch the pen gate and hope it didn't creak or screech as she opened it—and she had to let Whitestar know she was there without startling him. A few excited whinnies would awaken the ranch hands or the dogs. Somehow she had to prevent the colt from making a sound.

Tracy expelled a slow breath as she reached the gate of the pen. Now she could see Whitestar. He was standing near the center of the pen, dozing on his feet as if still on the alert for unexpected danger.

She called softly to the colt. Her voice was

no more than a whisper, but the colt's hearing was acute. He lifted his head and looked in the direction of the noise. Tracy could almost feel him tensing.

"Shhh," she whispered. "It's me. Quiet . . . don't make a noise." Tracy quickly unlatched the gate and slowly swung it open. It moved on its hinges without a sound. She slipped into the pen.

Whitestar was fully awake now. He'd recognized her voice, and came trotting toward her with an eager cry. Tracy gasped in panic and rushed to the colt. She placed her hand on his nose in a silencing motion. "Quiet . . . quiet . . ." she murmured frantically.

The colt nudged her in happiness, but made no further sound. Tracy's heart was pounding. That single cry might have been enough to alert the dogs. She had to act quickly. She gripped his halter with one hand and used her other hand to steady and reassure him. Moving as fast as she dared in the darkness, she led him out through the gate.

The colt immediately reacted to this new freedom. He pranced sideways a few steps, nearly banging the gate. Tracy gripped his halter tightly. "Easy, boy . . . please. We're going for a walk, but no one can know."

Whitestar gradually settled down, but a dog's bark suddenly sounded in the kennel area. A chill raced up Tracy's spine. She couldn't delay a second longer. "Come on, let's go," she whispered urgently to the colt. He understood her tone, and as she started off at a jog, he broke into a trot beside her. At the faster pace, his hooves thudded on the hard-packed earth, but Tracy had to risk the louder sound. She had to get away from the ranch buildings as quickly as possible.

The dog barked again. Beads of nervous perspiration broke out on Tracy's forehead. Her nervousness communicated itself to the colt, who gave a few grunts in his throat.

She tried to reassure him. "It's okay, boy . . . just relax." Tracy wished she could relax. The line of sheep pens had never seemed so long. The woods seemed so far away. She listened for sounds of life behind her—another bark, a door banging open. She chanced a quick glance over her shoulder. No lights in any windows.

"We're almost there, boy," she breathed. "Then I can turn on the flashlight, and we can see better."

Her eyes strained to find the spot in the woods where they could cross with the least trouble. If they entered in the wrong place, they'd have to fight through brush and fallen trees. But she couldn't see clearly in the darkness. The trees along the opposite side of the road were a shadowy blur. She had to take a chance and turn on her flashlight. She fumbled at her belt and pulled it free. Her hand was trembling, but finally she managed to flick it on briefly and direct the beam. She and Whitestar were moving too quickly. She still couldn't distinguish a clear path. She slowed him to a walk and flicked on the beam again. It reflected off some thick brush.

Tracy was so frightened, she couldn't think clearly. She took several deep breaths, hoping that would help. They walked several more paces, and she tried the light once more. Her sigh of relief was audible. The crossing was just ahead. She turned off the light and led Whitestar toward the woods.

The colt didn't like the idea of going into the thick maze of trees. He much preferred the brighter, clear course of the road. Tracy coaxed him on, but he balked. Then the dog barked again, and Tracy's patience snapped. "Come on, Whitestar," she ordered. "We've got to go. I'm trying to save your life!"

She got him past the first of the trees, then turned on her flashlight. The beam showed a winding course through thick clumps of trees, but the light made Whitestar more comfortable. Now that he could see where he was going, he went forward more willingly.

Tracy's heart was still pounding in fear and

dread. They were out of sight of the ranch house, but they still had a lot farther to go. She drew the colt forward, under branches, around trees, over rocks and fallen logs. If her mission hadn't been so important, she might have been afraid to be out in the woods alone so late at night. But she wasn't thinking of the dangers of wild animals. She was thinking about the dangers of the men who might follow behind.

Finally, they reached the path to the cabin. Tracy knew that route like the back of her hand. They were halfway there. She'd take Whitestar to the meadow and release him at the far side. The forests and mountains beyond would mean safety for the mustang.

The colt recognized the familiar clearing around the cabin. He pulled in the direction of the cabin door. To him the cabin meant food and a safe haven. Tracy could only think of the hours she'd spent there with the colt. She remembered how frightened he'd been the day they first brought him to the cabin, and how he'd gradually learned to trust them. She thought of the days of training him and playing in the meadow—and of all her dreams for him. She shook her head. Those times were over—forever.

Tracy tried to push the memories away before she started to cry. The colt would have a new life now, and a good life. He'd roam free, as he was meant to. And she'd be all right.

127

She'd have saved the colt's life—that was the important thing. She wouldn't think about how much she'd miss him, and how miserable she'd be.

"No, Whitestar, we're not going into the cabin tonight," she said in a voice strained by emotion. Tracy led the colt around the back toward the path to the meadow. Unconsciously she slowed her pace as they walked along. She wanted these final moments together to last as long as possible.

The meadow seemed bright after the darkness of the woods. Tracy paused at its edge and looked up to the star-spattered sky. Whitestar's rightful home was under those stars in a world where he could roam free and undisturbed by man. The colt sniffed the air and nodded his head, urging Tracy forward.

She let him lead her into the long grass. Her eyes scanned the far corners looking for any dangers, but nothing moved or stirred. She and Whitestar were all alone.

The time had come. Tracy couldn't stop the tears that welled up in her eyes. She threw her arms around Whitestar's neck and laid her cheek against his soft coat. "I love you, Whitestar. You've made me so happy, and I'm going to miss you so much! I hope you'll miss me a little bit, too . . . but not enough to come back. You can't come back here."

She wiped the tears from her cheek and

moved to the colt's head. She unbuckled the strap of his halter, then slowly drew it over his head. The halter hung limp in Tracy's fingers. Whitestar was free. She took a few steps forward across the meadow. The colt came along beside her.

Tracy turned toward the horse and kissed his nose. "Good-bye, Whitestar." Her words came out hoarsely. She felt like she was choking. "You've got to go now, boy. You've got to leave before anyone finds you. I won't forget you . . . ever!"

The colt continued gazing at her and nuzzled her shoulder.

"Don't you understand, Whitestar? You're free! You can go back to the other mustangs. Go . . . go on!"

The colt didn't move. With a sob, Tracy lifted her hand and smacked him on the rump.

He gave a startled, indignant cry, and trotted off a few paces. Only then did he understand that he was indeed free. He spun off and cantered around the meadow in sheer delight, shaking his head and giving playful bucks. His canter stretched into ever-widening circles. He was a sleek black shadow in the dim moonlight. Tracy watched him through her tears, memorizing his every movement, every line of his graceful body. Those memories would be all she'd have to comfort her in the days ahead. She'd wait and watch until he'd disappeared from view into the far woods.

But the colt missed Tracy's company. He paused and looked over his shoulder, then started back toward her.

At the same moment, Tracy heard noises behind her in the distance. The sounds were indistinct, but growing clearer. She'd been followed. The dog's bark had raised the alert.

"No, Whitestar—no!" she cried. "Go back. They're coming. They'll find you. You have to go!"

The colt didn't understand. He continued to approach. The voices were louder. They hadn't reached the meadow yet, but she didn't have much time.

"Go, Whitestar!" She waved her arms at the colt, but he thought it was a new game. He increased the speed of his trot and tried to circle around her.

"Tracy!" Her father's voice echoed up from the woods.

Whitestar heard the call, too. He stopped dead in his tracks a few yards from Tracy. His whole body tensed, and he flattened his ears against his head. Adult voices to him signaled danger. Yet he hesitated, so obviously torn between remaining at Tracy's side, and putting as much distance as possible between himself and those who would harm him.

Tracy knew that in another few moments, it would be too late. In desperation and panic she took the only object at hand—her flashlight—and flung it at the colt. He let out a terrified cry as it hit his hindquarters. He hadn't seen Tracy throw the light, but that pain on top of fear decided him. He cast one last look toward Tracy, then spun and galloped off into the darkness.

Tracy stood numbly, silently sobbing. She listened to the colt's muffled hoofbeats and saw him gradually disappear across the meadow and into the far woods. "Good-bye," she choked. "Be safe, Whitestar. I'll miss you."

She thought she heard his answering cry far in the distance, but it was drowned out by the voices and running footsteps behind her. She didn't even turn. Her punishment didn't matter. All that mattered was that Whitestar was safe.

"Tracy . . . Tracy!" The voices began to penetrate her misery. She suddenly realized that the cries weren't angry, but filled with worry and alarm.

Slowly she turned to find her brother, her father, and Emily rushing toward her. She squinted against the glare of their flashlights. Had Colin led them here?

Her father was the first to reach her side. To her amazement, he didn't scream or yell. Instead he put his arms around her and drew her close. "You're all right," he gasped. "Thank heavens!"

Colin and Emily joined them, but her father was the only one who spoke. "Oh, honey," he cried. "I'm sorry! I was wrong. All afternoon I tried to decide if I was doing the right thing. I felt rotten. I saw the way you were with that horse, and I saw how he was with you."

"Oh, Dad," Tracy moaned.

"Wait, let me finish. I couldn't sleep tonight. Finally I knew there was only one choice to make. I couldn't send off that colt. You were meant to have him. I've been letting something that happened years ago eat away at me. I shouldn't have. I went to your room to tell you . . . but you were gone. When we found out the colt was gone, too, we knew you'd tried to save him. Colin guessed where you'd taken him, so we set out up here after you."

Her father paused. His voice was filled with remorse. "I hoped we'd get here in time—but we're too late. You've let him go?"

Tracy bit down on her lip. "Yes . . . he's gone." Her tears started to flow again. If only her father had come to her sooner!

After a moment her father lifted her chin and looked down at her. "I'll make it up to you, sweetheart—somehow. Can you forgive me?"

Tracy's eyes were blurred by tears. "I guess you couldn't help the way you felt, Dad."

"But I shouldn't have taken it out on you kids. I should have thought about your feelings, too."

"It's—okay . . ." Tracy said dully.

Her father hurried on. "Emily told me that you and Colin have been learning to ride at Jason's. I think it's time you had your own ponies to keep at the ranch. I know it won't be the same as having that colt, but—"

Tracy's voice nearly failed her again. She knew how hard it was for her father to put behind his fears and make the decision he'd made. "Thanks, Dad . . ."

"We'll start looking tomorrow."

Tracy mutely nodded.

A horse's cry echoed across the meadow, high and clear. Tracy and her father turned toward the mountains where Whitestar had fled. Tracy knew it was the colt calling . . . perhaps saying good-bye.

Her father knew it, too. "Maybe that colt will come back one day," he said quietly.

"Yes," Tracy answered with a small surge of hope.

"At least he's safe out there now," her father added. "No one on this ranch will ever hurt a mustang again."

That news alone brought Tracy satisfaction. But her heart still ached. She'd never love another horse the way she loved Whitestar, but at least he was running free, as he was born to do.

And maybe someday he would come back.

About the Author

JOANNA CAMPBELL was born in Norwalk, Connecticut, where she grew up loving horses and eventually owning a horse of her own. She took riding lessons for a number of years, specializing in jumping. She's written three Sweet Dreams novels and the Love Trilogy in the Caitlin series for Bantam Books, and four novels for adults. In addition to her writing, she's sung and played piano professionally and owned an antique business. Seven years ago she moved to the coast of Maine, where she lives with her two teenaged children, Kimberly and Kenneth. *The Wild Mustang* is her second book for Bantam Skylark Books. Her first was *A Horse of Her Own*.

T·H·E SADDLE CLUB

Stevie, Carole and Lisa are all very different, but they *love* horses! The three girls are best friends at Pine Hollow Stables, where they ride and care for all kinds of horses. Come to Pine Hollow and get ready for all the fun and adventure that comes with being 13!

- ☐ 15594-6 **HORSE CRAZY #1** .... $3.25/$3.99
- ☐ 15611-X **HORSE SHY #2** .... $3.25/$3.99
- ☐ 15626-8 **HORSE SENSE #3** .... $3.25/$3.99
- ☐ 15637-3 **HORSE POWER #4** .... $3.25/$3.99
- ☐ 15703-5 **TRAIL MATES #5** .... $3.25/$3.99
- ☐ 15728-0 **DUDE RANCH #6** .... $3.25/$3.99
- ☐ 15754-X **HORSE PLAY #7** .... $3.25/$3.99
- ☐ 15769-8 **HORSE SHOW #8** .... $3.25/$3.99
- ☐ 15780-9 **HOOF BEAT #9** .... $3.25/$3.99
- ☐ 15790-6 **RIDING CAMP #10** .... $3.25/$3.99
- ☐ 15805-8 **HORSE WISE #11** .... $3.25/$3.99
- ☐ 15821-X **RODEO RIDER #12** .... $3.25/$3.99
- ☐ 15832-5 **STARLIGHT CHRISTMAS #13** .... $3.25/$3.99
- ☐ 15847-3 **SEA HORSE #14** .... $3.25/$3.99
- ☐ 15862-7 **TEAM PLAY #15** .... $3.25/$3.99
- ☐ 15882-1 **HORSE GAMES #16** .... $3.25/$3.99
- ☐ 15937-2 **HORSENAPPED #17** .... $3.25/$3.99
- ☐ 15928-3 **PACK TRIP #18** .... $3.25/$3.99
- ☐ 15938-0 **STAR RIDER #19** .... $3.25/$3.99
- ☐ 15907-0 **SNOW RIDE #20** .... $3.25/$3.99
- ☐ 15983-6 **RACEHORSE #21** .... $3.25/$3.99
- ☐ 15990-9 **FOX HUNT #22** .... $3.25/$3.99
- ☐ 48025-1 **HORSE TROUBLE #23** .... $3.25/$3.99
- ☐ 48067-7 **GHOST RIDER #24** .... $3.25/$3.99
- ☐ 48072-3 **SHOW HORSE #25** .... $3.25/$3.99
- ☐ 48073-1 **BEACH RIDE #26** .... $3.25/$3.99
- ☐ 48074-X **BRIDLE PATH #27** .... $3.25/$3.99
- ☐ 48075-8 **STABLE MANNERS #28** .... $3.25/$3.99
- ☐ 48076-6 **RANCH HANDS #29** .... $3.25/$3.99
- ☐ 48077-4 **AUTUMN TRAIL #30** .... $3.25/$3.99

Watch for other THE SADDLE CLUB books all year. More great reading—and riding to come!

Buy them at your local bookstore or use this handy page for ordering.

Bantam Books, Dept. SK34, 2451 S. Wolf Road, Des Plaines, IL 60018

Please send me the items I have checked above. I am enclosing $_____ (please add $2.50 to cover postage and handling). Send check or money order, no cash or C.O.D.s please.

Mr/Ms _____

Address _____

City/State _____ Zip _____

SK34-12/93

Please allow four to six weeks for delivery.
Prices and availability subject to change without notice.